METAL UP YOUR ASS

METAL UP YOUR ASS

PROTECTED BY THE DAMNED, BOOK 6

MICHAEL TODD   MICHAEL ANDERLE
LAURIE STARKEY

DISRUPTIVE IMAGINATION

METAL UP YOUR ASS TEAM

Beta Readers

Bree Buras
Dorothy Lloyd
Tom Dickerson
Dorene Johnson
Diane Velasquez

JIT Readers

James Caplan
Kim Boyer
Peter Manis
Joshua Ahles
Sarah Weir
Paul Westman
Micky Cocker
Larry Omans

If we missed anyone, please let us know!

Weapons Consultant

John Kern

Proprietor
Spurlock's - Henderson NV

Editor
Lynne Stiegler

DEDICATION

To Family, Friends and
Those Who Love
to Read.
May We All Enjoy Grace
to Live the Life We Are
Called.

— Michael Anderle

I t had been a month and a half since Stephanie and Katie had brought the idea of hunting unsuspecting demon assholes to Korbin's attention.

After the first one he was sold, though he still had his concerns.

The two girls had spent the majority of their time on this task, finding the demons and eliminating them where they could. They definitely had started to see a change in the way the rich were doing business, and politicians were up in arms. The word was out that these demons were being hunted, and they did not like that in the least.

Stephanie looked at the Golden Gate bridge as she and Katie walked along.

She loved San Francisco, even with its damned hills and constant fog. Katie could take it or leave it, and was only there for the mission: to take out a possessed California senator. He was more than just pocketing contributions. He was running the Senate like a personal bank.

He squashed his competition in every way, mostly because Big Business padded his pockets and pushed him to introduce bills that served only his interests. He was a scoundrel and a piece of shit, and he needed to be taken care of.

"So, after this you wanna go to Fisherman's Wharf?" Stephanie asked. "I understand they have great food... Hold up." She put an arm out. "We are here."

Katie peeked around the corner to find two tall, muscular bodyguards, their scowls letting her know exactly what they were out there for. They were both strapped, earpieces in their ears, and sunglasses on, even though it was night time. Katie turned back to Stephanie and nodded, then straightened her shirt and fluffed her hair. They turned the corner and sauntered up to the men.

"Ladies?" one of them growled, not breaking character.

"Possessed?" Stephanie asked, looking at Katie.

"*Yep,*" Pandora replied.

"We have confirmation," Katie replied.

"Aw, what a shame," Stephanie said, lifting her arm. "They are such handsome fellas."

She hit the first guy right in the nose, knocking his glasses to the ground. He grabbed his face as the blood flowed and glared at her with the red rings in his eyes shining brightly. He lunged toward Stephanie and the two rolled across the ground as they battled it out.

Katie looked at the other guard and smiled before baring her teeth and leaping onto his chest. She dug her knees in and swiped at his face, but she couldn't hang on and before long he had the upper hand. He threw her to the ground and pulled his gun. Katie swiped her leg up to knock the piece from his hand.

A little help here? Katie huffed as she asked for Pandora's assistance.

I might not always be here. Pandora yawned. *You need to learn to protect yourself.*

"OUCH, YOU FUCKING *BASTARD!*" Katie screamed, reaching up to her head.

The guard had grabbed Katie by the hair and lifted her to her feet.

Katie threw a punch, but it barely fazed the guy. She rolled her eyes and sighed.

She finally yanked out her knife and sliced his hand, forcing him to let her go. He hissed and moaned, holding his hand tightly as he glared at Katie with red eyes. She smiled and punched him in the nose as hard as she could.

He looked at her for a moment in confusion, then his eyes rolled straight back in his head and he fell to the ground with a thud. Katie bent over him as Pandora pulled the demon from his chest and sent it back to hell.

You're just mad at me because I wouldn't get the second dozen DONUTS, bitch. Katie wiped her bloody hands on the bodyguard's jacket and glanced at Stephanie, who was punching the other guard in the face as she straddled him.

The guy grabbed her wrist and slowly sat up with Stephanie in his lap, then flipped her over and held her down, growling and hissing. Katie shook her head and ripped a fence post out of the cement.

"You didn't even take the lady out for lunch," Katie bitched, shaking her head. "Where are your manners, asshole?"

She swung the metal rod hard at his head and he fell on top of Stephanie, unconscious. She struggled to roll him off her, breathing heavily.

"Thanks," Stephanie said, watching as Katie pulled the demon from his body and dissolved it. "He wouldn't have been a fun date at all."

"I just hope the Senator hasn't run out the back door by now." Katie frowned and helped Stephanie to her feet. "That would be a waste."

The two crept to the door and slowly opened it, pausing when they heard a man singing. Stephanie grimaced and raised her eyebrows at Katie.

"Is that *Queen?*" Stephanie whispered.

Katie shrugged and continued into the house, following the singing to a room where the senator was obviously taking some "me time." He had cucumbers over his eyes, a strange orange facial mask which was mostly dry, and Bose headphones pumping Queen into his skull.

Katie scratched her cheek and looked at Stephanie, who shrugged.

The girls flanked him and smiled.

"I wonder if he is imagining himself onstage right now?" Stephanie giggled, looking down at the senator. "That combover just flappin' in the breeze, makeup covering his face, tight leather pants with his belly hanging over the edge. You know, the real sexy stuff."

"He's got the mic in his hand right now," Katie continued. "He's singing into it, and he has a Steven Tyler sash tied to the stand."

Oh, for fuck's sake, Pandora growled. *Will you two fucking shut up already?*

Pandora reached from Katie's chest into the senator's and yanked his demon out. Both the senator and the demon screamed and growled.

Then the senator passed out.

Let's just kill him and go get dinner. I don't have time for you two to pussyfoot around, Pandora spat, dissolving the demon and sending it back to hell.

"*Someone* has her panties in a twist," Stephanie remarked. "We have time for one more before dinner. Come onnnn…it's a club just seven blocks away."

This is so annoying, Pandora grumped.

"Mmmm. Yeah, I'm up for another one." Katie agreed, taking one last look at the unconscious senator. "This time we should leave Eric in an alley, though. I'm sure he will love it."

Stephanie chuckled as they left the room. "Poor Eric. He always gets the short end of the stick."

"What else do we have to do other than fuck with each other?" Katie giggled.

They walked out the front door to be greeted by the moon over the bay, and Stephanie took a deep breath and skipped down the walkway to the street. Katie looked down at the guard who had given her such a tough time. He was groaning as he tried to pick himself up off the ground.

"Stay down there, buddy." She kicked him in the head.

He dropped again. "You'll thank me in the morning…or not. Either way, sweet dreams."

Derek sat on the cool cement floor, opening boxes and checking the contents off his list.

He was having a full nerd-out, excited to receive his computers so quickly. The new base was really coming along, and would be fully operational very soon.

Stephanie had put everything she had into getting the place going, whenever she wasn't hunting down demon-infested bigwig scumbags.

The team had made the base secure, erecting a twelve-foot-high chain-link fence with concertina wire billowing across the top of it that ran past the new buildings they were working on and was about three hundred yards out from the edge of the original compound. The rest of the area had been cleaned up and painted, and the new concrete pads had been poured. Derek was happy to be able to start his project. He had hoped a new computer workspace would be part of the move, and Korbin had not disappointed him.

"So, uh, what exactly is this whole thing going to do?" Calvin asked, pulling cords out of one of the boxes and looking at them in confusion.

"This will be a server room," Derek replied. "I've got three 72u stacks with multiple redundancy and three connections to the internet. It would have been smaller, but thank fuck the military was here before us. Korbin would have blanched at the cost of running cable out to the middle of nowhere."

"Okay," Calvin lifted an eyebrow, "but what does it DO?"

"It's surveillance, it's research, and it's operations," Derek said excitedly. "It's a window to the outside world before we set foot in it. All I need now are a couple of high-powered drones."

"Uh, where does this dongle go?" Calvin asked, standing up and looking around.

"God." Derek rolled his eyes and marching over. "That's not a dongle, *this* is a—"

"Hey, hey!" Calvin put his hands in the air. "You don't need to show me your bigger dongle. I think I'm good on that one."

"You are impossible," Derek replied, chuckling.

"Hey, you're the weird IT guy here, with your dongles, dingles, shafts, and whatever else you got hidden in those boxes." Calvin laughed. "Don't blame me."

The Seventy-Two were an enigmatic group of demons with their own structure and authority. T'Chezz might have been part of that Seventy-Two, but he was certainly not on the top rung.

The Seventy-Two were comprised of three levels, with each level having three sections of eight.

T'Chezz knew the math, and he also knew how difficult it was to work your way up the ranks. He was presently standing in front of several of the higher-ups, who were sitting around a large circular table in a leisurely fashion. This was his chance to pitch himself and make his future plans known. He was nervous—times like this were pretty much the only time he ever got nervous—but if he had these demons' support he could solidify the next steps in his plans.

T'Chezz looked at each of the five faces and, swallowing hard, moved forward, his big feet shuffling. When he reached the table he clasped his large hands in front of him and cleared his throat. Five of the eight prime-level demons were in the room, including Moloch, Asmodeus, Ba'al, Belial, and Azazel. None of them seemed very interested in listening to him, and T'Chezz knew there were several demons vying to move up the ladder right now.

"My plan starts out simply enough," T'Chezz began. "We'll infiltrate Earth by taking over as many human bodies as possible, then my minions will assume leadership of each of the countries. Once I rule the entirety of the planet I'll create a new hell, or like the humans say, 'Hell on Earth.'"

"That is very ambitious." Moloch leaned back and looked at T'Chezz.

"I agree." Asmodeus nodded. "Going against the entire world, even country by country, seems a bit ambitious. And why isn't Lucifer's wife with us, as she normally would for an interview such as this?"

T'Chezz looked at the ground, unsure what to say to that. It was true, she wasn't there. He had done his best to make sure she would never be at the table again.

There were multiple ways to climb the ladder of success.

"Perhaps she was not interested in hearing T'Chezz's plan," Moloch suggested.

Damn, Moloch was helping him. That was unexpected.

When he was successful, they would have no choice but to take notice of what he had done. It would be grand; bigger than anything the Seventy-Two had ever accomplished, and it would be something to hoist him up the ranks to where he ultimately wanted to be.

T'Chezz was in the second section of eight in the top level, and his goal was to work his way up to the top eight.

He knew through his sources that there were three seats open on the top level, and he deserved to be in one of them. He had served Lucifer faithfully for centuries by doing his bidding, keeping things tight and neat, and taking care of the loose ends, but he had become restless.

He wanted more. He wanted a seat at the table in front of him, and he was tired of just sitting around waiting for it to happen. He wanted more troops to command, more slaves, and a say in his own existence.

He would take what he wanted from the humans, including that bitch of a sister of his, and he would *make* the top-level demons give him his rightful place.

All he had to do at this point was figure out how to get around the new weapons. He still hadn't gotten his hands on one—or the maker, for that matter—and that posed a fundamental problem. This issue was becoming a serious thorn in his side.

And as if they could read his mind—and they might be able to—Ba'al spoke up just then.

"Humans are interesting creatures. I haven't been topside in a few decades, but I'm sure they haven't changed all that much. One thing they *do* have is gusto. Have there been any issues so far?"

"Actually," T'Chezz replied in a low tone, "one thing is giving me a bit of a problem."

"You aren't speaking of your sister, are you?" Moloch

sighed. "It would be a shame if she were to be your undoing."

"I am not worried about her. She is not an issue," T'Chezz told them, his eyes inadvertently flicking to an empty chair.

A chair that should be his. Irritation was building inside of him. "The humans have new weapons, something that injures the demon inside the human body. They can be lethal."

"*What?*" Belial looked at Azazel. "I thought we took care of *that* issue."

"Yes, well it seems they outsmarted us, Belial," Azazel replied. "I am not too worried. Humans tend to self-destruct."

"I find it concerning," Asmodeus interjected, "that they are fighting back. That's just what I didn't want to see."

"Well, boys," Ba'al yelled above their loud voices. "Let's just see what T'Chezz can do with this. I mean, it's better to know and plan accordingly than to not know. Right, T'Chezz?"

He nodded, feeling as if Ba'al's comment was more of a warning than an opportunity.

2

The alley was dark and smelled like sewage. It was just a fantastic environment for Eric, who was waiting for Stephanie and Katie to finish their mission.

"Stinks like rotten toe fungus in six-day-old socks." He was bitching up a storm. He still didn't understand how he had gotten roped into the whole thing.

Korbin hadn't wanted the women to go to San Francisco by themselves, so he had sent Eric to watch their backs. So far that had meant he had sat in dark alley after dark alley.

"Oh, yeah, sure. 'This won't take long. Why don't you just stay outside?' they said." Eric mumbled angrily to himself as he kicked an empty Mad Dog bottle toward the dumpster. "You forgot to mention it was fucking COLD in San Fran, Katie! And these alleys are goddamn *dark*."

Eric looked around for someone to confirm his grievances, but then remembered he was alone.

There weren't even any fucking cats back here, which said something. The rats were too ferocious for the cats to come after them for fucking dinner. He stared at the metal fire escape above him, which had water dripping from the railings.

There was a scream in the distance and Eric shook his head, shoving his hands in his pockets.

"This is pure and utter bullshit," Eric grumbled, pulling his cell out of his pocket and flipping through the screens. "I don't even have anyone to talk to. I thought this demon-hunting shit would be exciting."

He sighed, closing his phone and leaning against the wall.

It wasn't what he expected, sure, but it was a hell of a lot better than where he came from. At least he had a purpose now, even if it was being the lookout for a couple of wild demon hunters.

Just then another scream rang out, but this one was closer and louder. He straightened up.

The back door was flung open wildly and a man bolted out, screaming at the top of his lungs. Eric had parked the SUV at one end of the alley with the running lights on and he stood in the shadows of the other end—just in case. Whoever this was, he was heading straight for him.

Eric squinted down the dark alley to see more, but there was a shadow across the guy's face from the lights of the SUV behind him. He figured it was worth the risk of harming an innocent; as the guy moved closer Eric stepped out of the shadows and cold-cocked him. The screaming stopped immediately and the guy hit the ground like a sack of potatoes. Eric winced as he shook his hand out.

"Damn, dude, you got a strong jaw," he remarked, bending over the guy. "Let's see who in the hell I just knocked the hell out."

He rifled through his pockets, but he found nothing more than a comb, some gum, and two different pieces of paper with girl's numbers on them. Eric chuckled, crumpling the notes and throwing them over his shoulder.

"Sorry, buddy. You won't be using those to lure unsuspecting girls into your demon lair. What else you got in there? Huh…nothing? How you gonna call a girl without a cell phone?"

He reached into the guy's inner jacket pocket and pulled out a business card, but unless the guy's name was Cynthia and he worked at the Downtown Salon it wasn't his. Eric straightened up for a moment, dumbfounded that in today's day and age someone would go out without money, ID, or anything else, for that matter.

He bent over again to part the man's eyelids and shined his flashlight into his eyes, but there was nothing; at least, nothing that would peg him as demon-infected. No red rings, just a passed-out dude in the alley behind a San Francisco bar.

"Well, sorry, fella," Eric told the unconscious man. "Guess you were an innocent bystander. I have to say though, you got a set of lungs on you. I'm pretty sure they heard you screaming like an idiot all the way in Las Vegas."

Eric stood back up and tossed the guy's gum on his chest, looking around before grabbing his legs and pulling him behind the dumpster. The last thing he needed was someone looking down the alley and seeing a body.

What the girls were doing was already dangerous

enough. He didn't need extra attention because he'd knocked out some civilian who was probably taking cover from the girls inside.

The sound of glass breaking in the bar caught Eric's attention and he thought about going in, but he really didn't want attitude from the girls.

They had this. He knew it, but after knocking out an innocent person he felt the need to redeem himself by kicking demon ass. Still, he had promised to stay put. He knew one thing about Katie for sure: she had a reason for everything she did, even if it was to torture him and make him miserable.

After all, they were like brother and sister; it was her job to pick on his ass. He shrugged and walked to the SUV, reaching in and flipping off the lights. The moon was bright enough to see anyone coming out. He looked down at his watch and sighed.

"What the hell are they doing in there, anyway?"

"Come here, you rat bastard," Stephanie shouted, grabbing one of the possessed by the collar and breaking a beer bottle over his head. "I didn't come here for you, but I'll take you nonetheless."

Katie chuckled as she backed toward the bar. Two infected were eyeing her, and one took a step toward her. She wagged her finger at him.

"Nah ah ah," she taunted. "You know the rules."

"There *are* no rules," the possessed growled.

"Exactly." Katie coldcocked him as Stephanie ran up

and knocked the other guy over the head with a bar stool. Katie winced. "That's definitely going to leave a mark."

Stephanie walked over and grabbed a cosmo off the bar.

"Sooo, how was your day?" Stephanie smiled.

"Well, I..." Katie frowned as Stephanie took off after a demon across the room. "Hey, I wasn't done talking yet!" she called.

Katie shrugged and turned to the drinks on the bar. "Oh well, I'll just do a little taste test."

She moved down the bar, taking a sip of every drink along the way.

"Hmm, I give this one a seven out of ten. Good taste, terrible presentation," she commented, looking at the bartender, who was cowering in the corner. "This one, though..." She tapped the rim of the glass. "I have to say, you hit the mark, my friend."

"*Heads up!*" Stephanie shouted.

The bartender nervously nodded to Katie before jumping back as a demon-possessed flew over the bar, crashing into the wall and dropping to the floor.

Stephanie laughed and jumped onto the pool table, kicking a man in the face in mid-leap. She picked up the cue ball and chucked it across the room, nailing a red-eyed woman in the back of the head and wincing as she broke a table on her way to the floor.

"Whoops."

Katie moved down to another drink and wiggled her eyebrows at the bartender. She stirred it with the straw and took a sip, but immediately spat it out and wiped her mouth.

"Holy hell, what was that?"

"G-g-gin," the bartender stuttered.

"Oh, Christmas trees in a glass. Got it." She glanced at someone crawling across the floor, trying to stay in the shadows. "And who do we have here?"

The man, who was wearing a dress shirt and pants, crawled rapidly toward the back door. Katie walked forward and stepped on his leg, tilting her head sideways. The man straightened and put his hands in the air.

"Please," he whimpered.

That's him, Pandora told her. *And I can't believe you don't like gin. If you had the good kind, I promise it wouldn't taste like Pine Sol.*

I don't really want to spend the money to find out. Katie leaned down and grabbed the guy's collar. "Come here a minute, buddy, I want to ask you a few questions about the campaign contributions you've been taking over the last few months."

The guy whimpered, his feet dangling as Katie lifted him into the air. He didn't say a word, just choked on his own spit, terrified of what was going to happen. Katie sighed and shook her head, reaching into his jacket pocket and flipping open his wallet to see his ID.

"Yep, it's you all right, and I have to say, you take a good driver's license picture," she said. "Good for you, I just look like I have seven chins and I walked through a hurricane to get there."

A loud crash behind her made her cringe and the politician's eyes darted past her. Stephanie was still taking care of the riffraff—which was fun and all, but Katie's stomach was growling. Katie smiled at the guy and looked at

Stephanie, who was finishing up the last demon in the group.

"We got the rat," Katie yelled to her. "Time to go."

"I was just starting to have fun," Stephanie responded, breaking a pool cue over a barely conscious demon. "Just five more minutes. Please, Mom?"

"Nope. Pull them together for a fast extraction, then time to hit the road." Katie chuckled. "But first, me and this guy have a little bit to talk about."

"I *swear* I don't know what you are talking about," he whined. "I didn't take any contributions."

"Really?" she replied, pulling a piece of paper out of her back pocket. "It says here you took over a million dollars from a fund for sick kids. Well, that's just fucked up, but I don't blame you."

"You don't?" he whimpered.

"No," Katie replied, looking at him with red eyes. "I blame your *demon*."

"You are so theatrical." Stephanie laughed as Pandora's demon arm came out of Katie's chest.

Stephanie looked at the bartender to give her some backup, but all he did was pass out behind the bar. Stephanie pursed her lips and sighed, jumping down from the table.

The demon Pandora was sending back to hell screamed and begged. It really didn't want to go. When the demon was gone the politician passed out cold and Katie let go, letting him fall to the floor.

"Hey, where's my bartender?" Katie asked.

"He passed out." Stephanie jerked a thumb at the space

behind the bar as she sat down and started popping pretzels into her mouth. "I guess he couldn't take anymore."

"Too bad." Katie sat next to her and sipped the drink in front of her. "Humans these days! Oh, wait, didn't one run out of here earlier?"

"I got him." Eric kicked a body out of the way as he looked around. "Damn, you took out the whole bar."

"They wouldn't give him up." Stephanie shrugged and picked up a cherry. "You gotta do what you gotta do. How was alley duty?"

"Fine," Eric wiped the blood off a barstool with a napkin. "I think I now have rabies and tetanus, but hey—at least I'm alive, right?"

"So, are we off to dinner before Pandora has a complete meltdown?" Katie asked.

"Yes, I'm starving!" Stephanie jumped up and headed for the door.

"You guys go grab the car. I'll be out in a second," Katie told them.

She went to each of the unconscious possessed and yanked their demons out. Why the hell they had all chosen this establishment, she wasn't sure. Only two were merely human.

She walked back behind the bar and wrote a thank you on a napkin before shoving it into the bartender's pocket. She propped him against a stepstool and put a balled-up coat behind his head, then stood back with her hands on her hips and nodded in approval.

"Sorry, buddy. You were really brave there for a second."

Several cops busted through the front door with their guns drawn.

"Hey, hey!" Katie put her hands up. "I think you guys know me."

"Guns down, boys," the lead cop ordered. "It's the D Squad."

"Most these people are just unconscious now; all the demons have been removed," she told them, popping a cherry in her mouth. "This guy, though…he gets VIP treatment, you hear me?"

"Yes, ma'am." The cop chuckled.

"You boys have fun now, you hear?" She waved as she walked toward the back door. "Oh, and this one?" She nudged one comatose body. "He's a politician. A big one, but he won't be going back to the Hill for a while, most likely. I heard he voted against police raises anyway."

Katie disappeared out the back door, leaving the half a dozen cops shaking their heads as they stepped over unconscious bodies.

"All right, boys, spread out," the lead cop said. "We got a lot of people to see to."

"Damn!" one of the cops exclaimed. "This guy was punched in both eyes, and he is still holding onto his 'nads."

"Right, left, kick in the junk?" his partner asked, looking over his shoulder.

"Yeah, that's definitely my favorite move," the cop replied. "Poor guy is gonna be hurting when he wakes up."

"Wait!" His partner looked at the pool table. "Is that guy wearing a *tutu*?"

Everybody chuckled, moving the furniture around to

clear a way for the EMTs to get through when they got there. The captain walked into the place and looked at the guy in the tutu on the table, two pool balls placed right next to each other between his legs. He sighed and looked at the lead cop.

"Let me guess…the D squad was here." He chuckled through his long curly mustache. "At least they have style when they break up a bar full of people. How many were there? Six or seven?"

"Uh, no," the lead cop said. "It was just two of them. Maybe three, but we heard two female voices when we were coming in."

The captain let out a long whistle. "I need these girls on the force. Whip you idiots into shape. All right, get this mess cleaned up, I'll figure out a story, because I don't think the guy holding his balls is going to believe a gas leak made them pass out when he wakes up."

"Probably not," the lead cop agreed, holding back a laugh. "But the truth isn't very likely either."

"Too true." The captain looked around one last time before walking out the door. "None of this is believable anymore."

3

G eneral Brushwood looked out the window as his helicopter touched down on the landing pad.

A short skinny man with thick-rimmed glasses and a white coat stood next to two armed guards, waiting for the general to exit the helicopter. He sighed, grabbed his hat, and swung open the door. He hated dealing with the scientists; they were always so clingy and nerdy. Still, he was at Research Base 221 for a reason, and it wasn't the vibrant nightlife in southern Louisiana.

It was the main research base for the demon-related research. Demons were rife in the area.

The general stepped out of the helicopter and shook the scientist's hand as they hurried across the helipad. The general saluted the two guards at the entry to the building and was ushered inside, then into an elevator.

The activity that went on in the building was top secret, and most of it happened hundreds of feet below the surface. From the outside it looked like a normal office building, but that was just a façade.

"Doctor Dolt, it's good to see you," the general started as the elevator doors closed. "I expect you have been busy."

"Oh, yes," he replied excitedly. "Examining the demons' blood has been very educational."

"And what exactly are you looking for?" the general asked.

"Well, first we had to make sure that we understood the complexity of the human RBC, sir," he began, then noticed at the general's lifted eyebrows. "The human red blood cell, that is. Anyway, the RBC is biconcave, meaning that it has a disc shape to it; a discocyte, which can bend when going through our smaller capillaries. Now, we know our blood cells can be infected, and are subject to changes due to genetic deformations and the like. We started out by studying these with different testing devices and through controlled experiments. Then came the fun part: we redid all the trials and tests with demons' blood."

The elevator door opened and Dr. Dolt gestured the general into the hallway, walking quickly to catch up with him.

They took several turns through the long corridors and stopped outside a glass-fronted room. The general looked through the window at several scientists in all-white suits, who were doing various things including taking blood from possessed humans strapped to tables. These humans were the ones that couldn't be saved; the ones who had lost their reason.

They were starting to fully morph into their demon.

"Our specimens have been fantastic," the doctor said. "They have provided us with some really great samples."

"And what do you do with those samples?" The general asked as he squinted through the glass.

"Well, we run them through the atomic force microscope, we splice them with optical laser tweezers, and really, a whole slew of procedures. We subject them to normal twists and turns, and to abnormal external stress."

"And?" the general asked.

"Well, did you ever make a homemade lava lamp with oil and water when you were a kid?"

"Yes," the general answered.

"When the bubbles move up and down in the oil, they bend with the shape of the glass," he explained. "They are oblong and transparent, and they look like if you held them in your hand they would be harder on the outside than on the inside."

"Okay, sure," the general replied, understanding what he was hearing for the first time since he arrived.

"If you were to pump one through a tube, the bubble would conform to the shape of the tube and bounce back when it came out the other side," he explained. "That's the human RBC, only red in color and very small. Now, a demon cell is more of a jelly-bean shape. It doesn't conform as easily to a smaller space; it would stretch out. Over time, the human RBC, with the right pressure from the demon, starts to look like that."

The scientist pointed to a woman strapped to a bed. She was fighting the cuffs on her arms and her face was distorted: her mouth wide, her eyes bulging, and her tongue almost black. The tips of her fingers were dark like they had been frostbitten, and on the end were talons.

"Her cells are morphing her body," the scientist explained. "They will ultimately kill the human body."

"And trap the soul," the general muttered.

"Well, we don't believe in the soul here." The doctor chuckled. "But yes, in essence; it traps the human brain inside."

"How do we kill it?" the general finally asked, turning to the doctor.

"That's what we are trying to figure out, because that jelly bean—it isn't affected by outside influences," the scientist replied. "Not yet, at least. We are trying to find an injectable that will do the trick; something that once it is in the bloodstream, the demon dies. Of course, this will kill the human too, most likely. But the human is completely gone at that point anyway."

"So you are looking for demon cyanide." The general glanced at the woman again. "Kryptonite for the demons. You are trying to find a way to infect the infected."

"Precisely," the doctor said, relaxing a bit. "And when we do, we should be able to find a cure for the rest of the Damned; the ones who haven't been taken over."

"Right." The general nodded. "If that is even possible."

Joshua stepped out of his van and looked out across the new landscape. This was his new home; a feeling that he wasn't sure he liked. He had never been very good with change. His "issues," as his mom called them, or "gifts," as

Stephanie called them, gave him a bit of anxiety when it came to differences in his environment.

Still, he had fought demons, ferchrissake! He could handle a new building, especially knowing that all of his things were set up and ready for him inside. The place wasn't finished, but the base structure for his workspace was complete, and that was enough for him.

He could make it feel like home later.

Joshua looked at the two girls he'd brought with him and nodded, gesturing to the building in front of them.

They clapped and shouted, excited to get to work in the new space. He fumbled with the keys as he walked to the door, finally putting the key in the lock before entering the security code on the pad next to the door.

When the green light came on, he put his thumb on the scanner and waited to hear the door lock click. He turned the key and slowly opened the door, revealing a wide-open space covered in white tile. His equipment, shined up like new, waited for him.

He closed the door behind them and locked it again, setting his things on the table just inside. The girls walked around in awe, as if they were in a foreign land.

Joshua chuckled. He loved seeing that; it helped him feel like he wasn't the only one who was looking at everything like it was the first time.

"Check this out." Joshua smiled as he walked over to another keypad.

He pressed his code in and stood back as a hatch in the floor opened. Slowly a platform moved upward, filling the space. The girls frowned, unsure what the big deal was.

"Is that an elevator?" one of the girls asked.

"No. Gosh," Joshua chuckled, "I would never fit in there."

"Me neither," she said with relief. "Then what is it?"

"It will have the cabinet for the finished work on it," he explained. "We designed it to keep as much of our work underground as possible. Whenever I finish a piece I'll bring the cabinet up, load it, and send it back down for safekeeping in an underground chamber. It's not finished yet, of course. They are struggling to get through the shafts because of the ventilation, but it keeps us that much safer."

"That's brilliant." She nodded and bent down to look closer.

"Well, here we are." Joshua rubbed his hands together and headed over to his workspace, turning on the machines as he passed them. "Let's get to work. These demons aren't going to wait on me."

Calvin pulled the handkerchief from over his nose and mouth and squinted across the sandy plain.

It was a windy day out at the new compound, but they couldn't waste any more time, they needed to get things in place.

The fence was finished, except for the newly-implemented security system that would detect any movement around it, so he was out there helping get that in place. Demons were cunning; he knew that. The team wanted to utilize every possible precaution in case they decided to attack the new base.

Calvin looked toward the fence, which was about three hundred yards out. He lifted his binoculars, taking note of the small yellow flags sticking up from the sand along the corridor.

Those would help them identify the traps and weapons, but they blended in enough for a demon on the hunt to not notice them. Deep traps had been dug and lined with cement in various areas near the fence.

A board was then placed over the trap and covered with sand. Anything over ten pounds would fall right down into it, trapping the beast inside. They had made them large enough to accommodate several regular-sized demons or one very large one.

Closer to the buildings were pop-up machine guns, barely visible to the human eye.

The team could run out to the guns and lie in the shallow trenches behind them to aim the guns at their targets. Of course, these were all secondary protections. The entire point of the base was that demons wouldn't get that far to begin with. Korbin and Calvin were smarter than that, though; they knew that if they didn't prepare, they would be left unguarded just like last time. But here, the idea of being trapped underground with a bunch of demons was far too dangerous to ignore.

Calvin sighed and made his way to a tent set up next to Joshua's new space. He dusted the sand off his clothing and sat in a folding chair, grabbing a water from the cooler he had brought with him.

He took a sip, letting the cool breeze under the shaded tent wash over his sweaty skin. It was one of those things; a task that needed to be done, but the whole idea behind it was almost depressing to him.

He used to feel so safe and secure inside his barracks or compound—whatever they wanted to call it—but staring at those little yellow flags caused discomfort in the pit of his stomach.

He couldn't get past them. They were like doomsday flags waving in the wind…right in his front yard.

Damian climbed the stepstool and set a hook into the wall. He had brought his lighted cross to the new base for his chapel. He had a larger room this time, and the freedom to set it up however he wanted.

Sure, for him it was about faith, but it was also about creating a space that felt comforting and safe to the team, regardless of their beliefs. That was one of the things he had loved about the chapel at the old base; it had been a haven.

Even during the demon invasion, not a single book had been moved in that area. He wanted to achieve that same effect at the new base.

Calvin walked up behind him. "Hey, Cross Boss. Getting settled in?"

"Trying." Damian grunted; he was trying to find the hook while supporting the large cross, but he succeeded a moment later.

He stepped back down the ladder, plugged in the cross, and stood back smiling. Calvin sat down on one of the pews that had been brought over and took a drink of his water. Damian shrugged and sat down next to him.

"It isn't home yet, but it will be," he offered.

"You know what I'm waiting for?" Calvin asked.

"What's that?" Damian replied.

"I'm waiting for someone to *literally* burst into flames when they walk into your chapel." He chuckled. "I mean, you hear people say it all the time, but you're always left wanting, you know?"

Damian chuckled. "Though that would be interesting, I'd like to keep the space combustion- and ash-free for a bit."

"Well," Calvin announced after a moment's pause, "I gotta get back to work. I just wanted to check on ya."

Damian smiled. "Thanks."

His eyes followed Calvin as he walked out of the room and he sat there for a few moments, staring up at the lighted cross on the wall and thinking about how it would all look in the end.

He grabbed the bag he brought with him, pulling out several candles, a bible, and his cross. "Oof." He stood up from the creaky old pew, walked up to the front, and lowered himself to his knees.

Damian set up the candles on a table and lit each one with a small prayer. When they were all lit, he opened his bible and started a ceremony to bless the space. He went through the chapters and verses as he had been taught, but at the end he paused, not feeling like it was enough. Like it wasn't personal enough for this place.

"Lord," he added. "I pray You bless all of us, Damned and

non-Damned alike. I pray You make this a sanctuary for the house, a place where anyone can feel safe. And mostly, Lord, I pray You give us the aptitude, the speed, and the courage to kick those demon assholes right back to *hell*."

He nodded and started to stand up, but stopped.

"Oh, and thank you for your blessings, Amen."

4

"**D**id you see how that guy looked in that tutu I found hanging above the bar?" Stephanie laughed. "I mean, seriously…that guy is going to be so confused when he wakes up."

"Don't you think it's even the slightest bit mean, what you do to the humans left after the possession?" Eric asked as they reached the old base. "I mean, they aren't possessed anymore."

"This coming from the guy who knocked out a human and hid his body behind a dumpster." Katie laughed.

"That was an accident," Eric argued. "But I have to admit, the guy in the tutu was pretty awesome—especially with those pool balls between his legs."

"Right?" Stephanie wiped the tears from the corners of her eyes and took a deep breath. "Oh, sometimes this job is way too much fun."

"Yeah, for *you*, but since I was technically the lead in

this operation, I have to go brief the boss." Katie groaned as she got out of the SUV.

"Oh, you'll be fine. Just don't tell him about the dress-up." Stephanie giggled.

"Or me knocking out an innocent," Eric added. "That would get me taken right off this detail. Actually—"

"Nope, you are on it for life," Katie interrupted, patting Eric on the back as he walked through the doorway. "We will haunt you if you try to get out of it."

"The worst part is, I believe you." Eric waved to them and climbed the stairs.

"I'll see you guys in a bit." Katie headed toward Korbin's office.

"Good luck," Stephanie yelled.

"Right," Katie muttered to herself. "You got this."

Are you just a pussy, afraid of the boss-man? Pandora asked.

Can you stop with the p-word please? Katie griped. *It's so vulgar and gross.*

You think your pussy is gross? Pandora asked. *That explains a lot.*

Oh my God, stop! Katie grimaced. *Not mine, the word.*

All right, Pandora agreed. *Stop being a clam? Stop being a vagina? A vajayjay, a wet trap, a mound of pleasure, a—*

Just stop! Katie put up her hand. *Call it whatever you want.*

Then I shall call it "Henry," Pandora announced proudly. *So, stop being a Henry.*

You are impossible. Katie shook her head. *Do not call my vagina "Henry."*

You said I could call it whatever I wanted, Pandora argued.

Just be quiet, Katie replied, knocking on Korbin's door.

"Come in," Korbin yelled.

How about "Albert?"

Katie ignored Pandora and went in, the familiar smell of sweat and man mixing in her nose. She made a mental note to be as far from the training facility as she could get when she picked her room.

The last thing she wanted was to smell the gym all day long; that musky, damp smell that every gym had.

"I'm glad to see you in one piece." Korbin nodded to the chair in front of his desk. "Please have a seat. From the reports, you took out quite a few minor demons and two strong ones. That will be a nice payday for you and Stephanie."

"And Eric," Katie added. "He was part of the team, so he deserves something from it."

"Good call." Korbin made a note. "So, how did it go? Any problems?"

"Nope," Katie replied, picturing the guy in the tutu. "In fact, at the first one we took two demon guards down and found the target, who was covered in orange facial mask, belting out Queen. That one was pretty easy."

"Ugh." Korbin grimaced. "Early or late Queen? Demon or not, put him out of his misery if it was the wrong one."

"I know, right?" Katie smiled.

"And the second one?" Korbin asked, looking at Katie.

"It was pretty bad boss, I won't lie." Katie chuckled. "Seriously, you should have seen it. Stephanie was a monster in there. She wanted that asshole politician but no one in the bar would point him out, so what does she do? She warns them that she will kick *everyone's* ass until she finds him. Next thing you know, you have human and possessed alike lining up for a piece of her. I mean, some of these guys were huge, looming like two feet over her with biceps the size of her body. That didn't deter her; she kicked all their asses. I think she should be good on practice for at least twelve hours with the workout she had."

And what did you do? Pandora scoffed. *Drank Martinis and let me do the dirty work.*

"She *is* quite the handful," Korbin agreed. "Though I did get the report back from the police department." He looked down at his notes before his eyes looked up to Katie. "There is something in here about a man in a tutu?"

"I have no idea what you're talking about," Katie replied, sitting up straight. "He must have done it to himself. You know how crazy those demons can get."

"Yeahhh." Korbin rubbed his chin. "But apparently he wasn't possessed, just unconscious."

"How did you know that?" Katie asked.

"I didn't. It was a test." He laughed.

Tell him about the cosmo, Pandora grumped. *Oh, and the bartender you tried to hit on after he was already out.*

I did not, Katie grumbled. *I was thanking him for being subjected to our ridiculousness without running screaming out the door. How dare you!*

Even numbnuts took down a guy in the alley. Pandora scoffed. *I mean, he was innocent but he could have been a demon. If he was, Eric would be a bigger hero than you.*

Stop being so cranky, bitch, Katie snapped at Pandora. *Besides. I was back-up, spelled K-A-T-I-E. You may have sucked the demons out, but I'm telling you right now—I'm the one who got you close enough, especially after that little show you put on for the guards. You're lucky I didn't let myself get beat up.*

Um, yeah, I'm offended by the word bitch, so I'm gonna need you to change that up. Pandora snickered.

Fine, Katie replied. *How about "dickhead?"*

Katie went up the stairs, slightly embarrassed after Korbin had started laughing at her. He could tell she was in a fight with Pandora.

She really needed to work on that face of hers. People were going to start thinking she was insane, which wasn't that far off since her demon was a complete pain in the ass.

She walked into the living room, heading toward her room to relax before getting in some evening training. She had learned very quickly that when Pandora stepped back, she needed to not only tighten her body but the moves she was using as well.

"Hey, how did it go?" Eric asked from the couch, He was drinking a Coke.

"Okay." She put the back of her hand to her mouth as she yawned. "They put the tutu in the police report but not the guy behind the dumpster, so you're clear."

"Damn it," he moaned. "That was going to be my out."

"I told you." Katie smiled. "In it for life."

"Yeah, that's what they keep saying," he replied under his breath. "So what are you up to now? I'm going to go over to the new base and check on the hospital setup. You want to tag along?"

"Nah." She yawned again. "I am suddenly feeling too

tired for life. It's probably Pandora fucking with me again, but either way, I want a serious nap."

Damn right it's me, Pandora grumped.

"Okay." He sighed. "You should probably get some good shut-eye."

"I hope so," Katie replied. "I promise though...the next free night we have, we'll catch up on soaps."

"I will definitely hold you to that." He smiled, grabbing an apple and turning to the book in his lap. "Have a good sleep."

"I will." Katie smiled and went toward her room.

She walked inside and shut the door, pulling off her clothes and tossing them in the basket as she headed toward the bathroom. They had driven through the night to get back, stopping several times for food, which was another reason Katie couldn't understand why Pandora was so grumpy.

She brushed her teeth and pulled her long hair into a messy bun, then dragged herself toward the bed, falling face-first into the covers when she reached the end. She pulled herself up to the pillows and snuggled in with a content smile on her face, but as soon as she shut her eyes she opened them again with a look of irritation on her face.

Really? she asked.

Yep, Pandora replied. *I just shot up your adrenaline. You don't get sleep until I say so.*

What is your problem? Katie asked, sitting up in the bed and throwing the covers back.

You promised me something and you have not even thought about it, Pandora grumped.

Oh no? Katie demanded, jumping up from the bed and stepping over to her dresser. She grabbed some papers from the drawer. *Then what is this?*

Katie sat back down on the bed and spread out the papers she had taken notes on; they were all about the cars she was considering. Pandora cleared her throat.

Okay, I'm satisfied, she agreed, taking the adrenaline away. *Good night.*

I... Katie began, suddenly feeling totally exhausted.

Out she went, already lost in a dream world.

You're welcome, Pandora whispered gently.

———

Charlotte tapped the steering wheel to the beat of the music, humming along. She really loved driving, especially on a road trip like she had been on, hunting down info for Korbin's team.

The sun was just coming up, and she knew that she was getting close. She had driven all over the country since the last time she talked to Korbin, and it was time for a check-in.

She had spent so much time on this that she had completely stopped writing for the underground publication. She would probably start again, but it was a hard decision; she saw the world differently at this point.

Now Charlotte knew the truth—the actual truth, not just the conspiracies. People in her profession went their whole lives without finding out the truth about their stories, especially since most of them were made up. Now that she knew that truth, it would be a struggle to acclimate back into the world that she had known.

She wasn't that girl anymore, no matter how hard she tried to be.

The GPS directed her to take a left off the highway and down an old two-lane road she was pretty sure no one else would be using any time soon. She drove farther into the desert, finally seeing the top of a big tower in the distance. When she saw a sign she slowed down, reading it out loud to herself.

"Deviating from the path could get you killed. Explosion probable, blowing you into fifty-seven pieces or worse."

Charlotte snorted as she started toward the base again. "I mean, what could possibly be worse than that?"

She slowed down again, reading the next sign.

"It could be fifty-eight. That would be worse."

Charlotte rolled her eyes and shook her head, knowing they had put those signs there on purpose. At least they had a sense of humor.

She still didn't know how they held it together like they did. She was pretty sure she would be a basket case if she became Damned and had to join a mercenary team, or whatever they considered themselves to be. Finally she got to a pair of wide metal gates with a watchtower in the center. There was no one there, but the righthand gate slid open as she approached. She noticed the blinking of a small camera as she passed.

"Good cameras."

She drove to the center of the base and parked her car with the team's SUVs. She wasn't sure where the parking lot was, but she figured if they were parked there, she could too.

Charlotte put the car in Park and got out, shielding her eyes from the sun and looking around the compound. She could tell from the new cement and the smell of roofing tar and fresh paint that they had put some serious work into the place.

It was nice, and actually looked like a real military base. She turned when she heard a door shut and waved at Korbin, who was walking toward her, shielding his face from the blowing sand.

"Hey!" He shook her hand when he approached. "Let's go in the tent behind you and get out of the wind."

"Okay." Charlotte nodded, catching a mouthful of sand.

They walked into the tent and Charlotte looked around, watching the shadows created by the wind and sand beating against the tent. There was a small table and some chairs, so she followed Korbin over and sat down.

"You want a water?" he asked, reaching into the cooler to the left of the table.

"Sure," she replied, crunching sand in her teeth.

"How was your drive?" He handed her a cold bottle.

"Not bad," she told him. "I came from San Diego this time. I went home to take care of some stuff there while I was waiting for you to be available."

"Sorry about that." He nodded, opening his water. "This construction is taking up most of my time. I'm either here working, or I am in my office at the other base in the middle of the night trying to finish up the planning. It's definitely been an eye-opener, but in the end we will have a safe and secure place."

"I'm sure." Charlotte nodded. "I'm sorry about your other place. I heard there was a fight?"

"Yeah." Korbin sighed. "It was definitely rough, but most of us made it through. Now we are rebuilding stronger and better."

"That's all you can do," she offered.

"So anyway," Korbin replied, sitting up straight. "Tell me what you've learned, what you've heard, and anything and everything you've picked up."

"It has been a challenge, since I'm not Damned," Charlotte admitted. "The possessed know I'm not, the non-possessed don't care who I am, and all the people that I need to follow have shining red circles in their eyes. It has taken some serious reconnaissance."

"Hold that thought for just a second," Korbin said pulling out his phone and holding it in the air. "I want Katie and Calvin here for this…if I can get a damn signal."

Korbin made a note to have Derek install a signal booster—communications would certainly be critical in attacks—then stood up and walked to the opening of the tent. He finally found a signal and calling in the others. Charlotte sat quietly, entranced by the whipping of the wind against the white canvas walls.

She wanted to go home, but until she helped get this infestation under control she was destined for the bunker.

5

"Sorry it took me a second to get over here. We were putting in the last of the guns," Calvin offered as he walked into the tent. "Charlotte!" He went over to her, opening his arms wide. "It's so good to see you. How have you been?"

"Oh, you know, doing some black ops shit." She laughed as she gave him a hug.

"Charlotte was just about to tell us what she had learned from all her hard work." Korbin smiled. "She has been working harder than any of us."

Charlotte blushed. "I doubt that."

The three greeted Katie as she came in and grabbed a water.

"So," Calvin flipped the chair backward and sitting down, "hit us with it."

"Well, one of the things I found was a plot to infiltrate humans," Charlotte began, pulling out pictures of the demons she overheard. "I was chasing down a politician in

Arizona and happened to be standing in the right place at the right time. They were having a little meeting about it. It's going to take place out there. That's all I could find out, but I'm pretty sure if I go back I can find out a hell of a lot more, and maybe even get us into the event."

"Well, that sounds promising." Korbin rubbed his jaw, thinking. "That's great work, Charlotte. I would appreciate it if you did go back out there and see what you can dig up."

"Not a problem." She nodded. "I already packed a bag. Everything else I found out is old news to you guys. New to me, but that doesn't do you much good. I didn't realize this issue was getting so big, at least not until I heard about your base and what happened there. Then this news of the incursion, and my head began spinning a bit."

"It's ok." Calvin leaned forward, putting his hand on hers. "And if it ever gets to be too much, just tell us."

Her eyes opened in surprise. "Are you kidding me? I'm all about this." She laughed. "This is exactly the kind of reporting, minus the actual article, that I've wanted to do my whole career."

"Good." Katie stood up, waving her goodbye. "Then I wish you luck, and we will see you soon. I'm sorry to listen and run, but I have to get back to helping Derek before his head explodes."

"Me too," Calvin agreed. "But not Derek. I tried that IT stuff; not my cup of tea."

"Thanks, guys." Charlotte watched them walk back out of the tent.

She turned to Korbin. "I guess I'll hit the road then. At least get close before I have to stop to sleep."

"Before you go, I wanted to give you this," Korbin told her, pulling a thick manila envelope from under the table. "I'm sorry it's in cash, but we don't really have checking accounts."

"What is this?" Charlotte asked, cautiously accepting the envelope.

"It's ten grand," Korbin replied. "It's a bonus for all the hard work that you do for us. You have brought us, and continue to bring us, intel that is priceless, and it's not the safest job in the world. In fact, I guess it wasn't a job until I paid you. Think of it as hazard pay, but be careful how you spend it. I wouldn't put it in your bank account."

"Why not?" Charlotte looked at him.

"It's a red flag to the government," Korbin explained. "The government...they ignore the team's spending habits, but they won't ignore you. You are a subcontractor of sorts, and not on their radar. I think it would make things more difficult for you if you were. We don't work for them, but they like to act as if we do. Being technically deceased, we can get away with giving them the finger, but they can take *you* for all kinds of things."

"Yeah, I don't need that." She laughed. "Especially since this is my sole priority right now."

"Good. Just spend wisely. They won't really notice if you aren't writing checks or using credit cards. I mean, how would they?"

"You'd be surprised what they can find out," she answered, putting the envelope in her bag and rolling her eyes. "They probably know when I sing too loudly in my car."

"Um, good point," Korbin agreed, standing up. "I'll walk you to your car."

"Thank you." She followed him out of the tent and back to her hatchback.

He looked down at the young reporter. "I really want you to be careful out there, Charlotte," Korbin told her. "I don't like that you aren't protected."

"I am pretty good at sneaking around." She shrugged. "But still, I appreciate your worry. I feel like I'm actually contributing to something doing this, and it just *feels* right. Plus," she gave a flash of a smile. "you helped me find my family."

"I'm glad you feel that way." Korbin opened her door. "Now go on, and report to me at least every other day— even if it's just to tell me you're okay."

"Will do," she assured him, climbing into her car.

Korbin closed the door and waved as she pulled out and left the base.

He really hoped he heard from her again.

Why on earth are you up so early? Pandora groaned as Katie climbed out of bed. The sun was barely up.

Because we have a new vehicle to buy, Katie told her cheerfully.

Oh yeahhh, Pandora cooed, acting as if she had forgotten. *What are we getting? A Mercedes? An Aston Martin? A new Ferrari?*

None of those. Katie grabbed a tank top off her bed. *We are getting a Ford F-150 Raptor.*

We're what? Pandora asked, confusion evident in her voice.

Just hear me out, Katie replied. *This truck drove the Baja races through the sand, the rough terrain—everything. It was an 830-mile race, and when they were done they drove it back to base. They had stock tires on it, a stock engine, brakes... everything. The only thing they changed was adjusting the shocks slightly, because they had to put a roll cage on it for the race.*

Are we turning into racers? Pandora asked. *Because if we are, I'm making sure your zipper busts at the finish line.*

No, but we are now going to be living in the middle of the desert. And heaven forbid your brother decides to portal his ass back in. We will have a vehicle in which we can scream across the sand and knock him into the pits of hell without sending the truck along. Plus, we are saving a shit-ton of money by buying it. It's like less than fifty grand, and it will give us more power than any of the other cars we were looking into.

I don't know, Pandora griped. *It's a truck!*

Yep, Katie agreed, pulling on a sweatshirt and jeans. *And I bet we can drive one home today.*

Okay, I'll look at them, but if I hate them we will revisit this, Pandora said reluctantly. *It was* my *prize.*

It's a deal, Katie replied, just glad her demon didn't completely shut the idea down. *I really think you are going to like it, and there is no guarantee that one of those sport's cars would last, with the amount of sand and dirt blowing around on the new base. It would have sand in the engine the first day we pulled up.*

Well, take me to them, then, Pandora directed. *I won't know until you sit your pretty ass down in one.*

Katie left the compound before anyone else was awake, not wanting to give away what she was doing.

They took an SUV and headed to the dealership, seeing the Raptors all lined up nice and pretty on the lot. They pulled up just as they were opening, and a salesman came right out. This was definitely a different experience from Ferrari, but she liked the more down-to-earth crowd anyway—even if Pandora didn't.

"How are you?" the salesman asked. "I'm Tom, what can I help you with?"

"I wanted to look at the Raptors," she told him. "I am moving to a really sandy area, and I want to be able to travel anywhere I need to, even on sand and high ground."

"Well, the Raptor is definitely a good choice for that." He smiled. "We have eight in stock right now."

He walked Katie across the parking lot to the Raptor section. She wove between the different-colored trucks, finally opening a door and sitting behind the wheel. She definitely fit a lot better in the Raptor, and it felt safer than the vehicles she had tried out to that point.

Tom got the keys and they took it for a test drive, and Katie fell in love with it immediately.

What do you think? she asked Pandora.

I guess it will do. She sighed. *But you better show me one hell of a time out there on the dunes. I want to be peeing in your pants with fun by the time you're done.*

Yeah, maybe I should rethink this. Katie chuckled. *Or get some Depends.*

"What do you think?" Tom asked as they pulled back into the lot.

"I love it." Katie stroked the steering wheel and turned to him. "Do I need to order it, or can I buy one off the lot?"

"We have several with all the bells and whistles," he assured her. "Just depends on what color you want."

"Hmmm," Katie mumbled, thinking to herself. "How about dark red? That way they can't tell if it's bleeding."

Katie laughed to herself, but the salesman just stared at her with a blank expression. He didn't seem to get it, but then, he wouldn't. She cleared her throat and got out of the truck.

"Shall we?" she asked, glancing back at Tom.

He shook his head and lifted his eyebrows as he caught up with her. She smiled awkwardly at him as he held the door for her. He took her to his office and sat her down.

"Man," Katie mumbled to herself. "This is a tough crowd."

Tom looked at her. "The race red has almost all the upgrades, including the heated seats and steering wheel, the rearview assist package, sprayed bed lining and bed cover, plus the Raptor logo on the rear. The seats are plain leather, but we can get some with orange accents if you would like?"

"Ah, no," Katie replied. "Wow, boosted that to seventy thousand. Ok."

They went through all the normal paperwork, dotting the Is and crossing the Ts. Finally, she opened her briefcase took out a small pile of bills, setting it aside before she slid the case across the table to him.

He lifted an eyebrow and opened it, trying to keep from gaping.

"I don't like to use banks." She shrugged. "It should all be there."

"Right." He looked at her, then back to the cash. "It's Vegas. Not like this is the first time someone has won big, then bought a car." He looked up. "Which casino?"

"Aria," Katie lied.

Pandora snickered. *Wow, that lie rolled off the tongue like it was greased.*

I'm already lying, with my completely fake ID, I imagine it isn't a large penalty on top of that, all things considered.

Whatever. Pandora sniffed. *I'm just pointing out I haven't lost my touch.*

Tom interrupted their conversation. "I'll take this to the manager."

Katie had guessed they were going to check up on the money in the briefcase, but she didn't care; it would come back legit. When he brought her the keys she arranged to pick up her SUV later, and he showed her out to her new race-red Raptor with a dark shadow tint. It was all gassed up and ready for her to drive off the lot.

It still had some beads of water from their car wash.

She smiled and waved at Tom as she drove away, thinking about how he was probably happy to be rid of her.

She didn't blame him all that much. She knew she was slightly strange; even stranger to those outside her inner circle.

Katie drove straight over to the Pinkbox donut shop to celebrate their new purchase. She knew Pandora had been wanting to try their new cupcake donuts.

When they got inside Katie ordered her normal dozen,

and two cupcake-flavored ones. She bit into one and decided she liked it.

Pandora sighed.

What's wrong now? Katie asked.

It tastes like cake, Pandora told her. *I don't like it. If I wanted cake, I would eat cake. These are just lumpy round cupcakes with hard shells.*

I know. That's why it's great! Katie laughed. *Well, we have one left. Waste not, want not, and all that. I'll eat this one, then we'll switch over to our normal donuts. Is that okay?*

Yeah, I suppose. She sniffed. *I mean, people* want *to eat donuts, right?*

Yes, Katie replied.

Then why do they make donuts that taste like other things?

I don't know. Katie chuckled. *That's a good question. I guess we are all trying to make eating things like cake acceptable during breakfast.*

Sheeiit. Pandora scoffed. *If I ate cake for breakfast I would not be ashamed.*

I know you *wouldn't,* Katie griped. *It would be a little embarrassing for me.*

Get over it! She laughed. *Being embarrassed is life-limiting in the worst way.*

Pandora, can I ask you a question?

Sure, she said, forcing Katie to pick out the crème filled chocolate-covered donut from the box.

Why does it seem like you want to avoid going back to hell at all costs? Katie asked. *I mean, it's your home. You've spent centuries there, and while as a human I wouldn't want to go there, I do know how nice it feels to go home.*

Oh, you mean other than the whole dying part? Pandora asked.

I mean, I'm not really sure how you would die, Katie replied.

Oh, it can happen. Pandora chuckled nervously. *Typically it's a heavenly host and a sword you can't even see, but it can happen. They don't play fair in those situations, but at the same time, if you've got a heavenly host after you, you have done something far beyond the normal demon/devil mischief. You've obliterated an entire race, o...or...*

Taken over a planet of humans and forced them to do your bidding? Katie asked.

Uh, yeah, that would probably do it, Pandora admitted. *Just know that I am not immortal. There are ways to kill us; the secret just doesn't lie in human hands, that's all.*

Does a heavenly host come from God? Katie asked.

I really don't want to talk about this anymore, Pandora answered. *It's like us talking about all the ways you can die. It kind of kills the mood.*

All right, Katie agreed. She wouldn't press the issue, at least not right then. *What is your favorite dessert?*

I like tiramisu the best, Pandora purred.

Oooh, that's a good one. Katie nodded. *I like brownies. Not the crappy ones you get at a restaurant, but like the super-chocolaty gooey ones you make at home. Get them hot, cover them with vanilla ice cream, and I am in heaven.*

I like pot brownies, Pandora offered.

You would. Katie laughed.

What about a dessert that isn't made from a box? Pandora asked.

Oh oh oh, Katie exclaimed excitedly. *I know exactly what I like.*

It's about time, Pandora said snidely.

Churros, Katie stated.

Excuse me? Pandora asked.

Oh my God, you've never had a churro?

Uh, no? What is it?

Katie went into an entire explanation of how churros were made, where you could get them, why they were so popular, and most importantly, what made them so delicious. Pandora listened quietly, but Katie could tell she was drooling on the inside. She had to figure out where she could get Pandora a churro soon.

So, wait... Pandora said. *We are talking about a long shaft of sugary cinnamon-y goodness, with a caramel cream filling that I stick into my mouth and bite off?*

Oh God, Katie moaned.

Why have you not talked about this before? Pandora asked.

I'm realizing now that I shouldn't have talked about it at all.

It's like you have been hiding the perfectly-designed dessert. It's the right size, you bite it and cream comes out, the right girth... Wait, how big can they be?

6

K atie took the Raptor for a spin around Vegas before she headed back to the first base she had called home.

As she came up to the area where T'Chezz had come out of the portal, she veered off the road into the sand. There was definitely a difference between the Raptor and the Ferrari. In the Ferrari she'd had little to no control whatsoever, but in the Raptor she sped along like she was on the highway. When she reached the area where the portal had been she slammed on her brakes, coming to a halt right where she would have hit that bastard and knocked him into next Tuesday.

But would you attempt that in real life? Pandora asked. *I mean, he could have grabbed that bumper and taken you right down with him.*

I guess we'll find out next time he decides to burst out of a portal from hell, won't we? Katie answered, turning the truck around and heading back to the road.

Pandora sighed. *I'm starting to think I created a monster.*

Takes one to know one. Katie laughed.

Touché.

Katie drove back to the 15, swerving in and out of the sand, having a blast in her new truck. She realized it was one of the best things she had done for herself since she had bought the Ferrari.

She had been so busy demon-hunting that she hadn't bought anything for herself besides food, and that was usually for Pandora.

She was racking up the money, but it was just sitting there. The Raptor had cost her one big demon and a few smaller ones for the upgrades, and she was feeling like she was back in the saddle again.

When she pulled up in front of the base she revved the engine, catching everyone's attention inside. They all piled out of the house, oohing and aahing at her new ride.

She got out and smiled at Korbin, patting her truck on the side. He shook his head and grinned, watching Eric and Derek do circles around the thing. It almost got a better reaction than the Ferrari had, but then again, this was a group of men. Well, and Stephanie. Damian walked out slowly and smiled, looking at the bright-red truck.

"You got a new ride," he exclaimed.

"Yep," Katie said proudly. "I had a promise to keep, and with the new base the way it is, I decided to go with something I could do a little more damage with. The Ferrari was awesome, don't get me wrong, but I think I outgrew that stage. I walked right in and bought it off the lot."

"We are going to have to go take it out for a sand-dune

test drive," Calvin said, lifting his eyebrows. "Do a little surfing out there at the new place."

"You are going to have to let me drive this thing," Eric demanded, eyes bright.

"We shall see, young Padawan." Katie laughed.

They stood around talking about the truck for about ten minutes, then everyone shut up. The loud *thump thump thump* of helicopter blades echoed through the compound.

Katie stepped over to Calvin and looked into the distance as a helicopter came rushing toward them and swooped over their heads. Stephanie crouched, and everyone else backed toward the building in alarm. Korbin stayed put, though, standing next to Katie's truck as the chopper landed.

Katie stepped forward as the bird touched down, the propellers on top spinning just as fast as the two smaller ones on the sides. It was sleek and scary as hell, but as sexy as could be. It moved fast and sharp, and Katie had to admit it was awesome to watch. Korbin put his hands in the air and turned to the team.

"Your new airbus has arrived," he called.

"What?" Calvin chuckled.

"I figured it was time for us to upgrade." Korbin jerked a thumb toward the helo. "We can't keep driving to the airport, hoping to not run into traffic, now can we? The new base is farther away, and this baby will get us to the airport in fifteen minutes flat, if not quicker."

Everyone started talking loudly, excitement replacing the alarm they had felt just moments before.

They waited until the bird's blades had come to a complete stop and raced over to take a closer look. Katie stood at the back of the truck, just staring. She was excited, but she felt like Korbin had just stolen her thunder.

They really needed that bird, that was for damn sure, and she couldn't have imagined a hotter-looking helicopter to chopper the team wherever they needed to go. Korbin walked up next to Katie as the others gathered around the chopper, completely leaving her and her beautiful new truck behind. She looked at the Raptor and petted it like a dog, sticking out her bottom lip.

Korbin threw his head back and laughed, grabbing her shoulder and walking them toward the group. Calvin came up behind her and leaned forward to whisper in her ear.

"Sorry." He laughed. "That's a sweet-ass truck, there is no disputing that, but I'm afraid it's no Ferrari, and it's *definitely* not an X3."

"Is that what that thing is?" Katie asked.

"Yep," Calvin said, standing up straight and crossing his arms in front of him. "That is the Eurocopter X3, or 'X-Cubed,' as they like to call it. As far as I knew it was still experimental, but hell—Korbin can get his hands on anything. It goes two hundred and ninety-three miles per hour, and man, it can go forever."

"Why does it have propellers on the front?" Katie asked.

"Those are tractor propellers," Calvin explained. "Instead of it having propellers on the tail it has those, and they are gear-driven from the main propellers on top. That thing won the Howard Hughes Award, which is huge in the helicopter business. I'm just surprised the man didn't pick up the racer model, which is insane and uses like fifteen percent less fuel. This one will do just fine, though. It can climb over fifty-five hundred feet per minute. That would have been handy in Los Angeles."

"Yeah, it would have." Katie laughed. "I guess if I'm going to lose my fans to anything, it might as well be a badass helicopter."

"That's for sure." Calvin grinned.

Katie's eyes widened in excitement. "You think he'll let me fly it?"

"Not a chance in hell." Calvin patted Katie on the shoulder and headed toward the chopper.

"Well, it was worth a shot," Katie said to herself, shrugging.

She joined the others at the bird, and they gazed at its glory and took turns sitting in the pilot's seat. Korbin told everyone he was going to learn to fly it, and when he had his license he would bring another one of them into the pilot program as well.

He wanted to eventually have their whole operation run by members of the team, whether they were there or coming there to help. He wanted to keep the place as safe as possible, which was why he had invested in the chopper and was trying to keep the contractors as minimal as possible.

"We don't need strangers in our midst anymore," Korbin told them. "We need to stand united as a team, and we need to not feel the sting of loss anymore. We need to push through our training and get stronger and wiser, and this helicopter is going to be a great tool to help us defeat what's out there. This is a big step for us, one that will be scary at times, but I promise you it will all be worth it in the end. Now, I want everyone to go inside, change your clothes, and get ready for training."

Everyone groaned but jogged into the building, feeling the excitement of the afternoon. Korbin looked at Katie and winked, climbing into the chopper and looking over things with the pilot. Katie smiled at Stephanie, who had walked up and put her arm around Katie's shoulders.

"Hey, at least now we have a badass ride for our hunting." Stephanie looked at Korbin, then the bird.

Katie laughed. "I don't think Korbin is gonna let us take the chopper for that."

"No." Stephanie nodded. "Oh, hell no, he wouldn't. I mean, look at your new truck. The thing looks angry and ready to hunt."

"Hell, yes, it does." Katie pumped her fist.

"We can throw a bunch of demon-infested assholes in the back of that thing." She laughed.

"Just don't scratch the paint," Katie warned. "I'm leaving that for the next time I bowl over a demon and send him plummeting back into the depths of hell. I want to see what Ruby Red looks like on the front of T'Chezz. Maybe with that big-assed FORD emblem embedded in his chest."

"Me too, girl. Me too." Stephanie laughed and went into the building with Katie right behind her.

The general eyed the scientist.

"So you see, here we are studying demons' limits," the scientist explained. "We want to know their strengths and their weaknesses. Our biggest challenge is that all our demons are inside a human body. We haven't captured an actual demon yet. They are big and hard to contain, and getting them here would be nearly impossible, so we are working with what we have. Don't get me wrong—these demons are pretty unfriendly, but they are shielded by their human."

"So you are able to study them to a certain extent, but not fully," General Brushwood mused as they walked through the underground tunnels of Area 61 in northern Louisiana.

"Right," the scientist replied, as they approached the labs.

"What about a dead one?" the general asked. "Would that be sufficient?"

"It would be," the doctor agreed, "but as you may remember, when you kill a demon it either evaporates back to hell or turns to ash. We tried testing those, but that didn't show us anything. It was just ash under a microscope; nothing is alive in it."

"Oh, right. Well, I just don't know how we are going to—"

Right then a loud crash echoed through the corridor, followed by a scream. The doctor jumped in front of the general and shoved him through a door as a demon broke through the window and tumbled across the floor in front of them.

"He's broken loose," the doctor shouted, slapping the alarm on the wall.

The general pulled his gun, but before he could aim the guards pulled him to the floor. He looked at the ceiling as red laser beams shot across the hall, spearing the beast.

Small guns dropped from the ductwork , and alarms blared. The demon growled and looked at the general with a smile. He took two steps forward to lunge, but before he could complete the action the guns fired wildly. The beast flew back, gyrating with every hit. The guns kept firing, spraying bullets all over the hall and directly into the demon.

After what seemed like an eternity the alarms stopped, and the guards helped the general from the floor. He stepped closer to the corpse on the floor and watched as what was left of it slowly turned to ash. The doctor shook his head, ordering clean-up crews to take care of the mess.

"I want the other damned enclosures triple-checked!" the doctor barked. "If this one got out there might be a weakness in the security, and we cannot *afford* to lose another one."

"Wow," the general exclaimed, putting away his gun and straightening his uniform.

"I'm sorry, General. Please forgive us." The doctor straightened his glasses. "This seldom happens, but when it does we are fully prepared for it." He waved a hand toward the ash pile. "As you can see."

"What happens if there is a human in the hallway?" the general asked.

"That's why we earn hazard pay, General." The doctor smiled and patted him on the shoulder.

The doctor walked over to some of the other staff and start giving orders. The general couldn't believe they were so nonchalant about this.

On top of that, he had not been briefed on the security measures at that facility. Had he known, he might not have been so cavalier about pulling his weapon. He stopped one of the staff as they walked past.

"I'm sorry, I just want to ask a question."

"Yes, General." The man smiled. "What can I help you with?"

"If there was someone in the hall, maybe trapped between the demon and the wall, they would have been hit?"

"General, you have to understand the power of these beasts," the guy explained. "They can do more damage than bullets ever could. The system is made to kill anything in the hall. We can't be *too* careful. We cannot allow one of our people to be infected, and we cannot let a demon escape the facility. They are too wild and dangerous, and most are injured in some way. It would be like a rabid dog outside."

"I understand," the general replied. "Thank you."

"Sure." He smiled as he walked away.

The general took a good look at the hall. The walls were thick metal, everything was covered in some sort of protective gear, and even the security features had a plexiglass shield on them. He hadn't paid close attention before, but now he started to feel a bit uneasy about the whole thing.

He wondered if the first base he had gone to had that kind of protection. He was sure they did; they were an even larger facility than this one.

"Shall we move on with the tour?" the doctor asked, walking up beside the general.

"Sure."

The general followed the doctor down the hall, stopping for a moment to look at the other demons in their cages. They looked like wild animals: chained to the floor, the bars on their cages scratched and rough from their teeth and nails. He struggled to see the humans inside those cages at all.

"They used to be people." The doctor glanced at the demons. "We have seen some go from human to completely demon, but others came this way. Still, somewhere in them is the person who used to have that body. They are just too far gone to do anything for. You have to understand that, or you will drive yourself crazy."

"When all the humanity is gone, we will have lost," the general replied. "I damn sure hope that isn't anytime soon."

7

T'Chezz stood in the great hall, the hood of his long black robe pulled up over his scaled head. His red eyes gleamed vibrantly as he looked at the high arched ceilings. The building was reminiscent of something that would have been found on ancient Earth. The stone beams curved toward the center and had demonic enchantments etched into the craggy surfaces. It was the high assembly gathering place and its halls bustled with demons, some there for sport, others with actual positions in the levels. T'Chezz had been there many times before, but never for a meeting like the one he was waiting impatiently for. The rest of the top eight were away doing the master's bidding but Moloch was still there, and he had called T'Chezz in for a secret meeting.

T'Chezz and Moloch had never truly seen eye to eye, but they'd always had the same goal: to overtake the weak, to strive for success, to be the bigger demon. T'Chezz knew this was no peace offering, but his plans were big;

huge even, and if he succeeded, Lucifer would take notice. Moloch would want to be a part of that, to work himself up the chain. The higher-level demon had ambitions as well, mostly centered around standing at the left side of Lucifer. Moloch wanted to rule just below the king himself, and have everything that went along with that. Demons were gluttons for glory and power, and Moloch was no different than the rest.

"T'Chezz," the demon growled, walking toward him. "Thank you for coming."

"Thank you for the call," T'Chezz replied.

"Shall we go to my office?"

T'Chezz nodded, putting his hands behind his back and walking beside Moloch. As the lower demons passed they put their heads down, paying respect to the mighty demon. He was feared, which was not the same as respect, but the outcome was no different. He was revered by the strong, feared by the weak, and used as a model for the ambitious. In reality he wasn't much stronger than T'Chezz, but he was an opportunist, knowing exactly who to schmooze and when.

"I hope we weren't too brutal on you during our last meeting." Moloch smiled, showing T'Chezz into his large office. "Your ideas are big, and we like that."

The fireplace was huge. It stretched along one whole wall, and though it looked like flames burned inside, when you looked closer you could see the tiny souls trapped in their own personal hell. They shimmered and flickered like fire, and T'Chezz made a mental note to get one of those.

"Do you like it?" Moloch asked as T'Chezz peered at the fireplace. "It was a gift from his Eminence himself. I think it's a bit showy, but who am I to refuse my own personal soul-catcher?"

"Right." T'Chezz chuckled, taking a seat.

"So, you are probably wondering why I called you here," Moloch began. "I'll just cut to the chase and not waste too much of your eternity. It is time I receive sacrifices again, and I am willing to offer them to you to support the over-throw of Earth."

"That is…unexpected," T'Chezz admitted. "Thank you. I would accept such help."

"Tell me, then," Moloch continued. "Where and why are you having the difficulties you are facing now?"

"The hunters have gotten smarter," T'Chezz explained, after a moment of thinking what the catch would be for accepting help from Moloch.

Any way he looked at it, the risk was worth it.

"There are no longer small rogue groups, they have militarized. And they aren't fighting with fists and swords anymore, our own demons are fighting us. They are called 'the Damned;' infected by a demon soul that is too weak to take over the human completely. The human harnesses those powers and fights with them."

"They can't be strong demons, then," Moloch mused.

"They aren't," T'Chezz replied, thinking of one in particular. "At least not all of them. But the humans have something that I can't nail down. It is a new weapon forged of magic and steel, and it gravely injures and even kills demons big and small. That, coupled with the train-ing, and the humans have become a bit of a force. My sources say they are no longer just waiting for a fight, either. One of them specifically hunts down the demons in the most influential positions and sends them back to hell."

"Well, well, well." Moloch chuckled, steepling his fingers. "Those fleshy little bastards are getting smart. I have to say, it's about time, it's only been a few fucking millennia since they could put two words together."

"Yes." T'Chezz snorted. "But it's a pain in the fucking ass."

"Here is what I'm going to do for you." Moloch leaned forward. "I will work on a counter-weapon, something that can stop them in their tracks. It can possibly even give them a little taste of their own medicine, and remind them that they are not all that smart."

T'Chezz grinned. "I like how *that* sounds."

"Good," Moloch replied, sitting back in his chair. "Can you get these killer soldiers of yours to show up so we can test this new weapon on them when the time is right?"

"That won't be a problem at all," T'Chezz assured him. "That's one thing I never had a problem with: getting the bastards to show up."

"Excellent." Moloch nodded. "Then go; prepare. I will do the same. I will help you get over this hurdle so you can continue your siege of the humans. Don't screw this up."

"I give you my word," T'Chezz responded, standing up.

He left without another word.

If Moloch wanted all these idiots in one place, he would make it happen. It shouldn't be that hard; he would just need to recruit the right demons for the job.

He was determined to see them dead, if it was the last thing he did.

The music at Torn Asunder was loud, and the sounds of ripe conversation, glasses clinking, and laughter blasted Katie as she walked back in from getting a breath of air.

The smell of food and stale beer was familiar and comforting, and she laughed as she watched a fight land in a plate of freshly-prepared nachos to the left of her.

The fight ended as cheese sprayed wildly into the air and those involved hugged in a gooey embrace, putting their hands up for the crowd to cheer them. Katie just shook her head, realizing that the bar she used to feel lost in suddenly felt like home. She had been doing this demon thing—head down and full speed ahead—longer than she had thought she would.

When she'd first arrived, there was a big part of her that had figured she would be dead within the first six months. She couldn't lie to herself about that.

But here she was, stronger than ever, striding through every day with a renewed sense of self. She walked back to the table and sat down with Stephanie, Damian, Calvin, Derek, Korbin, and Eric.

They looked like they were having a good time. Eric and Derek were scanning the crowd as usual, Stephanie was poking at Korbin, Damian was reading a book and sipping a whiskey, and Calvin was on the dance floor. He had a whole group around him, jamming to the early-nineties dance music pumping through the speakers. Katie laughed, watching Calvin hanging out like he was a normal dude enjoying his downtime.

"You guys are sooo boring," Stephanie whined, dancing in her seat. "Come on, old grumpy Gus—let's go cut a rug."

Stephanie stood up and put her hand out to Korbin, who slowly looked up at her. Katie put her hand over her mouth and leaned forward on her elbow, trying to hide the amusement she felt watching the two of them.

Finally he sighed and took her hand, letting Stephanie drag him onto the dance floor. Eric joined Calvin, seeing his chance to get in on the horde of women dancing with him.

"Whelp!" Derek smacked him on the back. "I think I'm gonna play some pool."

Katie chuckled. "No wild dance party for you?"

"Me?" Derek laughed, standing up from his chair and glancing at a sweet brunette in the corner who was giving him the eye. "I think I'll find my comforts somewhere else. Besides, I dance like Korbin."

Katie looked at Korbin, who was swaying side to side and clapping his hands. She burst into laughter, covering her mouth and shaking her head as Derek walked away nodding.

She took a sip of her beer and let the last giggle out as she looked around the room. Damian hadn't noticed anything and kept his nose pressed into his book. Katie wondered if he actually read the thing, or if it was a distraction from the evils that threatened his priesthood. She sighed and put down her half-empty glass.

What's wrong with you now? Pandora griped.

Nothing, Katie replied. *I was just thinking about how it would be nice to maybe have a guy for something other than a brother.*

Hallelujah! Praise Jesus, a miracle has come to us today, Pandora intoned in her best reverend impression.

Are you allowed to say that? Katie chuckled.

Hell, yeah, I am, Pandora snarked. *If old priesty-head over there can drink whiskey and swear, I can praise that fluffy guy in the sky.*

I'm not saying I'm ready to go cartwheeling into someone's bedroom, Katie pointed out. *I'm just saying a little romance never hurt anyone. Well, that's not entirely true, I suppose. Romance is probably the biggest cause of pain for humanity, but still.*

I would say it's number three on the list, Pandora told her. *One being death, because let's face it—none of us get out of this life alive. Except me, typically.*

Because you're not alive, Katie replied.

Pandora brushed her off. *Details. Two would be money, because it makes your little world go around, and third is romance.*

You have a point. I've come to terms with death and I have plenty of money. Katie laughed. *But that doesn't mean I don't think about that third one.*

You need to do more than think, girl, Pandora commanded. *You need to push up those tits, swivel those goddamn hips, and start showing these men who you are.*

I am pretty sure if I push my tits up any more than you already have they're going to stab me in the eyeballs, Katie replied.

Pandora kept babbling about picking up men, and Katie instantly regretted telling her how she felt. She tuned her out, staring across the floor at Stephanie and Korbin. They were talking and laughing, sharing the intimacy that Katie was starting to long for.

It wasn't just about sex for her. It was about having someone there. Someone to laugh with, cry with, get angry at, and all the other things that happen when you enter into a relationship with someone.

She wanted to be wanted, and she wanted to want someone back.

Every single morning Katie woke up wondering if it would be her last rise and shine. She went through her day thinking about the next incursion, not the next date or the next girl's night out like most of her friends.

She didn't sit around and drink bottles of wine at night. She planned out the next demon hunt with Stephanie, eating pizza and wiping her face on her sleeve. She could call herself a tomboy, but it was her life, not her personality.

Katie sighed and picked up her drink again, figuring that whatever was going to happen, she wanted it to happen organically. She didn't want to force it. She was not on the hunt; not for a man, at least.

She had bigger things to worry about, like the demons who were hunting her.

———

T'Chezz tapped his large scaly fingers on the desk, shaking the cup of pens on the edge. The underling demon kept his eyes on the floor, the wall, or anywhere else he could put them to avoid staring into T'Chezz's deep-red gaze. The big demon had a plan; something he had to get done, and he couldn't sit around and wait to make it happen.

"You understand what needs to be done, correct?" T'Chezz asked.

"O-oh, yes," the underling stuttered. "Y-yes, I understand what I have to do. I just don't understand why."

"You don't need to," T'Chezz growled. "Just know that you need to follow through, and the order comes from way above even my head."

"Yes, sir," the underling replied meekly.

"I need you to understand something," the demon growled. "I need Moloch's help in this. You cannot screw up, because if you do, everything I have worked toward for the last three centuries will have been for nothing.

"Moloch was the one who took care of the demon-killing swords the last time they came around, and I need him to do it again. I know he can; it just takes a little bit of research and the perfect timing. As far as your first task... Well, that is a favor for a favor. Something I knew I would never get this deal without."

"Yes, sir." The underling nodded. "I won't fail you."

"See that you don't," he growled. "You may go, but stay close for when the time is right."

"Yes, sir," he agreed, jumping up and running out of the room.

The servant stepped to the side as the demon ran by. He shook his head, put his hands together, and looked at T'Chezz. The demon rubbed his face and groaned, hating that he had to rely on an underling like that to carry out the dirty-but-very-important work.

"Are you all right, sir?" the servant asked.

"Oh, you know... Just trying to take over an entire planet, making deals with shifty Level-One demons, and trying to keep my head on straight." He groaned. "Why can't you be a mercenary and not a servant?"

"I don't know if I'd be much good at it," he replied.

"Honesty, I like that," T'Chezz grumbled, standing up from his chair and walking over to the window.

He crossed his arms and looked out over the hellish scenery, watching the souls floating in streams of lava. Thoughts of his sister flashed through his mind, and he clenched his fists a little tighter.

"I will make this work," T'Chezz decreed out loud. "Even if I have to kill every last human being on Earth."

8

K orbin sat at his desk, staring at the stacked boxes.

He was ready to move completely over to the new base and stop having to shuffle through everything like he had been doing. Just when he thought he was clear to pack something, he had to pull it all back out for one reason or another.

It was irritating, and the entire reason he had hated moving when he was in the military. Hurry up and wait, and while you are doing that, please unpack your bag fifty million times because you forgot and packed your toothbrush in the bottom.

At least he had a filing system this time, unlike his bags. They just held all his belongings shuffled up together. He thought about the old days; his time in the military, and the friends he had all but forgotten over the years.

The phone rang loudly, jolting him from his thoughts. He sighed and rubbed his face. He almost hated it when the phone rang nowadays. He never knew who was going to be on the other end.

The last thing he wanted was to talk to the general again.

"This is Korbin," he answered.

"Hey, it's Charlotte," a happy voice chirped.

"Charlotte." Korbin smiled, relieved. "How are you doing out there in Arizona?"

"Sweating to death." She laughed. "But good otherwise. I got an invitation to the next suspected incursion, and it is a huge one—the one I was talking about. They are focusing their efforts on women specifically. I got us four tickets."

"That's good work," Korbin replied. "I'll send Katie, Stephanie, Ella, and probably Amy from the other team down there."

"Well, I want to go," she said quietly. "I mean, that's what you pay me hazard pay for, right?"

"I don't know." Korbin leaned forward. "This could be really dangerous for our team members, much less a civilian with no formal training."

"I know the demons. I know who they are, what they look like, and what their plan is," Charlotte explained. "I am *vital* to this."

"All right," Korbin agreed reluctantly. "But you have to get out of there at the first sign of a battle."

"I will."

"Okay, I'll call you with the details of the others' arrival then. Stay safe, and good work." Korbin hung up.

He sat there for a minute before picking the receiver back up and dialing John's number in New York.

If Charlotte was going to put her ass on the line, he was

going to send a badass team of women. He couldn't afford a fuck-up on this one, not with so many civilian women attending on top of Charlotte, his spy.

Their lives were the most important thing. Second was finding out just what was going on with these demons.

"John," Korbin said happily when the man picked up. "How is New York?"

"Same old, same old." He laughed. "How about you? How's Vegas?"

"Quiet." Korbin pounded his fist on the desk three times. "Knock on wood. But I do have an incursion that requires a very specific team. I was hoping you would let me borrow Ella for a few days. This one is important, and I have some really good sources telling me that things are about to get really nasty out in Arizona."

"Uh oh," John replied. "Of course. I'll ask, then send Ella. Do you need anyone else?"

"No, I'm pretty sure these three women will be more than enough," Korbin said with a smirk. "I'll have teams on backup just in case, though."

"All right, I'll have Ella meet the other two in Arizona. Which city?"

"Phoenix and I will take care of the transportation from there," Korbin replied.

"Great," John finished. "Talk to you soon."

Korbin hung up, glad he had gotten someone Katie and Stephanie could trust to fight beside.

On top of that, he was told that Ella was a pretty damn strong Damned. They thought she might just catch up with Katie one day.

Korbin doubted that, but he wouldn't mind having two

Katies—not with the way everything was going. So it would be Charlotte, Katie, Stephanie, and Ella taking on God-knew-what, with an unknown number of demons and a bunch of innocents.

The whole thing made him more than a little nervous, but he would have to trust the girls' ability to handle any situation.

Ella was new, but not *that* new anymore. She would have to get to the point where she could jump on a plane at a moment's notice and head out to wherever she was needed.

Sink or swim.

She would be with friends, though, and Katie and Stephanie could protect her if need be. Charlotte was his real worry; an innocent among the others, wanting to help and being strong-minded. Those things could get you killed when you were completely inexperienced.

"Phoenix?" Ella laughed and looked in the mirror at her hair, which no longer showed any crazy colors. It was just long and black.

She was still *her* though: dressed in black, ripped jeans, nose ring, and worn out, scuffed boots. Training and the life of a killer had mellowed her a bit, but she channeled all that energy into being as badass as possible.

She took the black leather cuff off her wrist and threw it on the dresser as she turned to John, who was standing in the doorway.

"With who?" Ella asked.

"Katie, Stephanie, and some reporter who is a spy for them," John answered. "It's a special assignment; an event that's going to get crashed. A spa retreat for a ton of innocent women they are planning to infect. They need you, and wanted you to be the fourth."

"I don't know how well I'll fit in undercover, but if there's a chance for demon-slinging I am sure as hell ready for it." Ella pursed her lips. "Besides, the girls haven't seen what I can do now. I kind of want to show off my new mad skills."

"Right." John smirked. "Well, I'm sure they will be impressed, and you might even learn something new from them."

"Yeah." Ella smirked back. "Or maybe I'll teach *them* a few things."

"Umm, yeah, sure." He chuckled. "Just pack your things. You are meeting them in Phoenix."

"Sand and sun, oh yeah." Ella smiled. "I hope there's a pool at this joint so I can work on my tan."

"Mmmhmm," John said, walking away. "Said no goth chick *ever.*"

She yelled, "I'm not *goth!* I am just expressive of my inner soul, which is dark and gloomy." Ella looked at herself in the mirror. "He'll see; they will be super impressed by my skills. I'm stronger than they give me credit for. Bring on the big boy; I got this."

Ella packed her bag, hiding in the back of her mind the fact that she would be happy to see Stephanie and Katie again.

Perhaps more Katie than Stephanie.

She had settled down there in New York, but Katie and

Stephanie were the ones who had trained her and really shown her what it meant to be a demon hunter.

Every time there was a bulletin with news of tributes, she checked to make sure the girls were okay. She just hid the emotion underneath, trying to keep her wall up with the teams. She couldn't help but feel that those girls were her sisters, and she was stoked to fight alongside them.

Are you ready for this? Melneck asked.

Fuck yeah. She scoffed.

You know you aren't those girls. You aren't even close yet, Melneck reminded her. *So don't go marching in there, guns blazing and doing something fucking stupid. I don't need a one-way ticket back to hell, and I am pretty sure you aren't ready to keel over and die.*

Ella shook her head. *I'm not gonna die. But I'll tell you this right now: your cousins, the ones trying to fuck things up—they are going to meet their ends at the tip of my sword.*

The sun was shining brightly over Wickenburg, Arizona, a town just sixty miles from Phoenix.

It was dry and desert-y and had about six thousand citizens, mostly ranchers and those who ran the local Western Museum and the plethora of touristy shops centered around gunslingers and cattle drives.

Up in the rocky cliffs behind town, a gate creaked open and Moloch stepped out. He looked relatively human; shrouded to keep the humans from running off.

The sky crackled above him as his foot touched the sand, and dark ominous clouds rolled right in. He had come on a mission, but he was gonna make a statement while he was there.

Those who knew and worshipped him would see the signs, and the rest had better just keep out of his way. He walked down the dusty path toward the town, his boots crushing the sand.

He was in a human form as a disguise, but it was one huge man who covered the monstrosity that was Moloch.

As he moved the storm followed him, bright bolts of lightning crashing across the sky. He slammed his fist against a green sign on the side of the road marking sixty miles to Phoenix.

Moloch knew what was going down there in just a few days, but right then all he was worried about was creating his weapon; the weapon that would gain T'Chezz recognition and him a pat on the back. He'd be one step closer to Lucifer's left hand.

As he passed the Western Museum he growled and sent waves of energy at the front, which slammed the doors shut. People scurried about expecting it to start pouring any minute, but this wasn't a rainstorm.

It was a storm of enormous evil. He would deal with his project here, then move to the Northwest.

That was the more interesting project, and the one that would cause these humans fits.

———

Back at Demon Central, the staff were busy conducting research, directing teams to calls, and, most importantly, monitoring the energy of different areas to make sure no spikes in activity occurred.

The monitoring room was dark. The techs sat at their computers staring at their screens and listening to signals on different frequencies. The day had been quiet. In fact, the entire week leading up to that day had been slow.

A burst of energy showed up on the map and a soldier quickly lifted his hand.

"We got movement here," he called. "Audio and visual!"

The colonel looked over and frowned, then stood and made his way to the man's desk. They didn't usually get readings that strong. When they did, it often turned into a historical event. The teams were spread so thin, though, that this incursion may not have ended up on their priority list.

"What do you have, soldier?" his superior asked when he got to the desk.

"It looks like an incursion, probably upper northwest corner of Utah," the soldier pointed out. "There is a ton of activity over there. I'm not sure I've seen that many demons in one place on our map before."

"We need to put out an APD," the colonel directed. "Whitestaff?"

"Yes, sir?" The soldier stood up and saluted.

"I want you to put out an All Points Demon alert to the entire western area and the main command," the colonel instructed. "We need our teams and the private teams to know about this one. I know the military teams would struggle to get all those suckers."

"Yes, sir," Whitestaff replied, sitting back down.

He started to type frantically, sending the alert to each

corner of the map. Details were scarce, but they couldn't just let this one go by. The colonel opened the small black box on his desk and put the key in, turning on the switch. It was a signal to all commands to let them know a call was coming in. The mercenary teams didn't have that technology, but the colonel knew they monitored the military feeds for action. It was always in the back of their minds that their troops just weren't equipped well enough for the massive increase in demon incursions.

It wasn't long before the colonel's phone rang, and the general was on the other end. He sounded put out but concerned, and the colonel hated giving him bad news. It was unavoidable though, and he had known that from the moment the soldier caught the surge. Another call and another round of dead or infected soldiers, and that was just during simple calls.

"What's going on?" the general asked. "What is this APD about this time?"

"General, sir, there has been a massive surge detected in Utah, sir," the colonel explained.

"What is the target?"

"We don't know the exact target, sir," the colonel replied. "The specs have been sent to your laptop. Unfortunately the energy transfer was heavy but short, so we were unable to get a direct fix."

"All right." The general sounded annoyed. "Then how big is the area?"

"We have narrowed it to a ten mile by ten-mile area, sir." The colonel flinched, staring up at the large screen in the front of the room that displayed the map.

"That's a hundred fucking square miles," the general

replied angrily. "We'd be better equipped to try and hit a fly's dick with a dart while it was in flight than to find the demons in an area of that size."

"Yes, sir," the colonel responded. "We are working on narrowing it down."

"Do it, and call me when you have a better idea," he directed. "We don't need our troops just wandering the fuck around out there. That's how mistakes are made and soldiers get killed."

"Yes, sir." The colonel winced as the general hung the phone up angrily.

He stood there looking around the building. Everyone was working as fast as they could. The general just didn't understand that their equipment wasn't nearly as capable as it needed to be. They had only militarized demon hunting in the last decade, and tracking them was a lot different than tracking human enemies. There was no heat-seeker to find the bastards, and there was no way they could move as fast as the larger demons.

The battle already felt lost, but he hoped somewhere out there the mercenaries were tracking closer.

9

"I thought *Vegas* was hot," Stephanie said fanning herself. "Arizona is like Nevada on steroids."

"I like it." Katie smiled, looking up at the sun and taking in her Vitamin D. "I hate being cold. I feel like Korbin keeps the base at twelve below zero, so anytime I can heat up these bones I'm going to take it."

"You think Ella will be different?" Stephanie asked, watching the planes landing and taking off. "I mean, obviously she'll be different, but I am hoping that whole bratty bitch phase has ended."

"I think she will be Ella," Katie mused. "And if that includes bratty bitch, we will just have to take it in stride."

"Then expect me to try and knock it out of her," Stephanie commented.

Just then the door to the hangar opened and Charlotte walked in, looking rested, trendy, and way different from the underground rat Katie had originally met when she was first infected. She waved and walked over, giving Katie a big hug and a kiss on the cheek. She nodded at Stephanie.

"We are still waiting for one more, right?" Charlotte asked.

"Yeah. Her name is Ella. She's pretty green but she works in New York, so she should have some good skills," Katie explained.

"She was kind of a pet to us." Stephanie sighed. "She came in wild and wooly, I can tell you that much."

"So did I." Katie laughed. "So did you, actually. It's not about the way we came into this world. It's about what we will do to avoid being taken out of it, and Ella has that on lockdown."

With those words the front of the hanger slowly slid open, revealing a slick jet on the other side.

The jet came to a stop, and the crew prepared the stairs for deplaning. Katie watched with bated breath as Ella appeared, long black hair cascading down her back, a tight black tank top, and those ripped black jeans with worn-out boots. She was exactly as Katie remembered her.

"Hey, bitches." She smiled and put her arms up as she descended the stairs. "I'm *baaaack*."

"And a sight for sore eyes," Stephanie said, hugging her tightly as soon as she reached the bottom.

"So what's up?" Ella smiled, looking at Charlotte. "You must be the spy."

Charlotte laughed. "More like an investigator than a spy."

"Right." Ella chuckled. "Well, it's nice to meet you. I'm Ella."

"Charlotte," she replied. "Glad to have you on the team for this."

"All right, let's get to our next spot." Katie led the women out of the hangar and into a secured building.

They climbed the steps to the roof and stepped out onto a helicopter pad. Ella and Charlotte's jaws dropped as they stared at the chopper Korbin had sent for them to use. Ella pulled out her phone and snapped a picture of the bird, quickly sending the message she had open.

"Who are you texting?" Stephanie asked patronizingly. "Hopefully not a civilian; this is top-secret."

"No civilians." Ella smiled. "I'm showing my boss John the bird. I bet we get a helicopter inside a month now. You know how competitive he can be, especially when it comes to his fucking toys."

They climbed into the helicopter and put on their headphones so they could talk.

Ella talked about the last couple of months: the training she had gone through, and how absolutely ready she was for the mission. When that was done, Charlotte brought them up to speed on the details.

"We are going to a spa event in Phoenix," Charlotte explained. "From what I've learned, all the women will be untarnished. The goal of the demons is to get in there and change every human they can. They are obviously building an army of some sort. If we can successfully infiltrate it, we can get rid of the demons and save as many human lives as possible. Once that's done, we can squeeze some info out of the demons who directed the whole thing."

"Sounds good," Katie replied. "But just to clarify, we

don't know the exact location yet, how big the incursion is going to be, or even the type of operation we are in?"

"Right," Charlotte replied. "Think of it this way: it's good practice for those harder situations."

"Yeah." Katie scoffed and looked out the window. "Just what I need in my life...*more* surprises."

Do you know anything about this operation? Katie asked.

Don't have a clue. The Los Angeles one I had heard about in really early planning sessions at a round-table meeting. It was T'Chezz's deal, so I ignored a lot of the info.

Katie stared at the ground below them and listened as the girls talked. They were flying much lower than the jet did, but that crazy chopper soared through the air like a car; even smoother. They would be at their check-in point in no time. Then it was just getting settled in, because like most reconnaissance missions, they were going to have to be glued in one place.

"Are you're ready to kick some more ass?" Stephanie asked Katie, grabbing her attention.

"Yeah." Katie turned back to the ladies. "But this time *you* cannot dress anyone up. No tutus, I mean it. We don't need the press coverage."

"That was you?" Ella pointed to Stephanie and then Katie. "We all heard about a politician in a bar, and how two team members went through de-demonizing the lot, leaving one of the guys tied to the pool table wearing a tutu and cradling two pool balls between his legs."

"That was her." Katie pointed at Stephanie. "I just stood back and watched the carnage. It was like being in a movie, watching as the main character went nuts. I was definitely impressed, then I caught the politician and chaos ensued."

"You guys are nuts." Ella laughed, shaking her head and turning to the window.

"You have no idea," Katie whispered to herself.

The general raised his weapon and fired six shots at the demon running toward him, which fell before it reached him and turned to dust. He was in the middle of a two-team takedown in Texas, kicking demon ass and taking some names as well.

He had been in the service for a very long time, but still had the aim and fury he'd had when he'd served in the Sandbox. Just then three demons burst through the doorway and the general fired in their direction. He hit two of them and realized he was out of ammo.

The other fire team lit them up. Probably forty rounds hit three bodies before they stayed down.

"Goddamn it," he grumbled, ducking behind a table and pulling out another clip.

His phone rang and he growled, pulling it out and holding it to his ear with his shoulder. It really wasn't the best time for a chat, but he knew that the colonel was supposed to be calling him back with news on the APD that they had put out without much information behind it. He cleared his throat and pushed the clip into his gun.

"Colonel, what did you find out?" he asked.

"It's a clean-and-sanitize operation, General," the colonel called. "We have a one-mile radius now, and there are two teams on their way out there as we speak."

"Good. I... Hold on a sec."

The general could hear a demon sniffing around behind him, so he grabbed the phone with his left hand and spun to fire three bullets into the demon's skull. It shrieked so he shot it once more, watching it finally fall. He nodded and put the phone back to his ear, waiting for the demon to turn to dust before continuing.

"Sorry about that, Colonel. We are just wrapping up the incursion out here in Texas," the general explained.

"No problem, sir," the colonel replied.

"So two teams are on their way out there," the general repeated. "Do any of the mercenaries know about this?"

"Not that I am aware of, but they are not required to check in with us," the colonel replied. "As far as I know they don't have any teams in that area, so I am hoping our men can get in and take care of it before they can mobilize."

The general's backup nodded; everything was clear.

"Right." The general stood up. "Just remember: you can think of them as a powerful tool. It's not a competition. If you need their help, have the lead officer on the incursion call some of them in for back up. We all fight for the same cause. We just are a little bit more structured."

"Understood," the colonel replied.

"Call me whenever you have an update," the general ordered. "I have a bit more here, then I'll be heading back to my quarters at the base here. I'll be available on my cell."

"Yes, sir," the colonel replied, and terminated the call.

The general shoved his phone into the inside pocket of his jacket and left the building. He looked around outside, watching the medic giving care to some of the wounded.

Nobody had been killed. Nobody had been infected and

it seemed all the demons had been disposed of, so the general counted it as a successful venture.

Just as he was about to turn toward his car, a demon crashed through the door of the building. The general sighed and pulled his gun back out, waiting for the demon to get into range as it ran toward him.

The beast was hit by three different shooters simultaneously.

"Dumbfuck," he mumbled, pulling his trigger twice. The demon hit the ground face-forward and slid up the walkway until his claws were in front of the general's shoes.

He watched as the beast burst into ash in front of him, then turned his attention to the gun in his hand, feeling the warmth of the barrel on his skin. He shook his head and shoved it back in the holster, clipping the snap over the top.

"We need better fucking weapons," he grumbled to himself.

"General, are you all right?" the lead team officer asked, putting his hand on the general's shoulder. "We saw what was going on from the sick bay area. We appreciate you guys traveling out here. It really lifts the troops' spirits." He nodded to the pile of ash in front of the general. "It helps to see you inside, sir."

"What kind of leader would I be if I stood on the sidelines?" the general asked. "I have to get my hands dirty in order to fully understand what our soldiers are going through; our strengths and weaknesses, and everything in between. Besides, it keeps me young and on my toes."

"I'm sure it does." The officer smiled. "Why don't you

come and get some chow with us? It's nothing special, but I'm sure they would love that."

"I would, but there is another incursion going on and I have to get back to the base to get up to date on the intel." The general smiled. "Tell your men they did good work today. They made me proud."

"Of course." The officer nodded as the general turned toward his car.

The truth was he didn't give a shit about eating with them, nor did he want to be subjected to "chow." He did need to get back for the information, but mostly he wanted to get back to his normal work instead of fighting in the fields. He took two steps toward the car, but stopped when he heard the colonel call out to the teams.

"All right, Team Two! Load up. we have bodies to get out of there," he yelled.

The general turned around, confused. "Colonel, I thought that there were no casualties?"

"No *military* casualties," the colonel confirmed. "However, there were civilians in there when the incursion began. Some were turned and are unsavable. Others were demon lunch. There were fifty-two civilian casualties in the back quarters of the building."

The general nodded, angry at what he had just heard. The driver opened the door for him and the general climbed in, rubbing his hands together.

When the driver shut the door, he stared out the window at the soldiers carrying stretchers and body bags inside the building. He pulled out his phone and called Colonel Jehovivich.

"General," she answered. "How did the incursion go?"

"We got them all, and there were no military casualties," he told her. "But the civilian casualties were very high."

"I'm sorry to hear that sir," she replied. "At least you were able to neutralize the threat."

"Yes," he mumbled. "Still, I don't want casualties. It just feeds them."

"Understood, sir," Jehovivich responded quietly.

"We need more information on those mercenary blades. I'm afraid the time for niceties has passed. We are losing people right and left, and if our soldiers aren't as well equipped physically to handle the demons, then we need something to help us lower these casualties."

"I will look into it right away," she told him.

"Good. I will call you from the base when I get back."

"Yes sir," she replied, hanging up.

He put his phone in his lap and nodded to the driver, who slowly pulled away from the building and off the property. The general watched the Texas scenery from his window, thinking about the incursion in Texas and the one in Utah.

He wondered how many fatalities they would sustain, and he wondered if they weren't possibly going about everything all wrong. What he needed was time with Katie, the demon hunter who'd had something to do with the incursion at Korbin's base.

He knew there was more to her than what he was being told, but what it could be he didn't know.

Sometime later they pulled into the base and parked, and the driver helped the general out of the car. He was exhausted, but he wouldn't sleep until he got news of the Utah event.

There were lives at stake in that game, and the demons were taking everything they could. It was no longer good enough to kill a demon. They had to start thinking about long-term survival.

He needed better weapons, and he needed them yesterday. He wasn't sure if the mercs' blades were the key to stopping this surge of demons; he needed to find out more.

These battles had reached the point of survival of the fittest, and he did not like where his side sat on that scale.

10

Stephanie, Katie, Charlotte, and Ella had been at the retreat for three days. They went to the classes, taking turns watching for any sign of the demons.

Katie was in pure hell, never having bought into the tranquility bullshit.

There was constant "calming music" in the background, even in their rooms, and barely anyone spoke outside their quarters.

Katie told Stephanie that she needed to be the one talking with Korbin unless something very operation-specific came up. Stephanie wasn't sure why, but didn't question it.

That evening after dinner and their meditation, Stephanie grabbed her phone.

"Awwww, you aren't supposed to have that phone," Ella teased. "One of the yogis might just sentence you to a yoga lesson and meditation session if you aren't careful."

"Yeah, I have to work." Stephanie rolled her eyes.

"Korbin needs an update; it's been three days. I'm going to go wander through the enchanted gardens, puke on one of the fairy statues, and call Korbin."

"For fuck's sake, tell him to send donuts," Katie grumbled. "Pandora might mistake my kidney for one if I don't do something soon."

"Uh, that's gross," Stephanie exclaimed. "Get it together."

Stephanie left the bedroom and made her way through the building, nodding at the various people walking down the hall. Unlike Katie, she was kind of enjoying the peace and quiet—but definitely not the food. The cuisine was three out of the four complaints she kept hearing over and over.

She went through the back doors into the flower garden, turning on her phone and pressing a speed-dial key.

"This is Korbin," he answered.

"I think we might all just become yogis and say fuck this demon-slaying bullshit," Stephanie told him, looking around to make sure no one would see her and report her to the prison guards. "I mean, really…it's so quiet here."

"You'd be back in one day." Korbin chuckled. "You crave the loud and busy."

"You may be right, but I think a place like this might be good for you. Loosen you up a little bit." Stephanie giggled.

"I think I am loose enough," Korbin replied. "So, nothing so far?"

"If you don't count the issue with Katie, it's been serene and peaceful here," Stephanie told him. "Which is enough to make you hand yourself over to the demons anyway."

"What's wrong with Katie?"

"I guess it's more Pandora than Katie," Stephanie explained. "Pandora is on a donut-rager, and I am pretty sure she is about to bust out of this namaste prison and go eat some actual food that doesn't have any type of grass in it."

"Food is that bad, huh?" Korbin laughed.

"It's not bad, per se. It's just fucking incredibly healthy for you." Stephanie scoffed. "If we ate like this all the time, we would be the most in-shape group of demon-slayers on the planet. But we don't, so the rest of us are left with stealing a car and breaking out, heading over to McDonald's, or start eating the reporter."

"Poor Charlotte," Korbin chuckled. "How about Ella? Is she behaving?"

"She is pretty much the only one enjoying the food. They love her. She can't get enough of the bean sprout-and-dirt sandwiches."

"Uh, what?" Korbin replied. "Ella was the last person I thought would actually enjoy anything they had to eat there! She has the biggest mouth, too. I figured they might have kicked her out by now."

"Nope, well behaved and enjoying the stay," Stephanie explained. "Of course, it helps that her demon has found her reward center, and he's all about healthy eating. She says it's literally like she has a mini-orgasm every time she puts healthy food into her mouth. I've never seen someone her age eat so much broccoli."

"Well, that is definitely interesting," Korbin replied, slightly embarrassed.

"I am jealous. That's like the best diet idea ever,"

Stephanie commented. "To orgasm over vegetables and protein shakes? I'd rule the women in California with an iron fist and long stalks of celery."

Korbin skipped a response and worked on changing the subject. "What about everything else?"

"Oh, you mean the mission we are supposed to be on?" Stephanie looked around. "Yeah, that one. Not so much. Not a single demon has even set foot in this place. Not even a random demon wandering in by accident. We are starting to go stir-crazy."

Korbin was quiet for a moment, and Stephanie let him consider their options. "Do you think you should come back?"

"No, not yet," she replied. "I feel it. It's coming, so I just think we need to wait it out. I might not be able to keep Katie and Pandora sane for that long, but it will be easy to break out to get food and come back if it happens."

"All right." Korbin sighed. "Go ahead and wait it out, but call me again if anything changes."

"Will do, boss." Stephanie pressed End.

She stood there in the garden for a second. With the music pumping from the speakers, she felt like she was in a scene for a really hokey romance novel. She shivered, shoved her phone in her pocket, and jogged back to the building.

She could deal with the grass for dinner, the classes, and everything else, but she couldn't deal with feeling like they were getting fleeced—and that was exactly how she felt.

When she got back to the room, Katie was upside-down on her bed, Ella was slurping asparagus down while moaning, and Charlotte was in the corner reading.

They needed to stay there to save these women, and hopefully they could keep it together long enough to make it through the fight. Stephanie sighed and sat on the edge of the bed next to Katie. She looked miserable; injured, even.

"I can't believe she is eating more of that shit," Katie grumped.

"If it gave you an orgasm with every bite, would you at least try it?" Stephanie laughed.

"Yeah, maybe you're right." Katie sighed. "I need to make a donut run, though. Otherwise this bitch is either going to get really loud or silent, and it's bad news either way."

Moloch stared at the woman behind the counter as she rang things up. He tore the tag from the sweatshirt he was already wearing and handed it to her, and she ran it over a piece of glass on the counter. It made a beeping noise and Moloch looked around, confused. He hadn't been in a shop for decades, and definitely not one with so much human technology. The girl looked up at him and smiled.

"That will be one hundred and forty-three dollars and sixteen cents," she told him.

"You will give them to me for free," Moloch ordered, flashing his eyes to put the human girl into a trance.

"Here you are, sir. Thank you for your time here at

Bogarts. Come again," she droned like she was reading a script.

Moloch smiled and walked out of the store carrying his bag of clothes. He stared down at the sweatshirt he had on. There was a very large H on the back, and on the front, there was a cartoon version of Lucifer. The sweatshirt read, *I never get lost, because everyone tells me where to go*. He loved his new clothes, and the boots he had gotten were a lot more comfortable then the dress shoes the human had been wearing when he took his body.

He turned the corner and headed through the town to the residential area. As he walked through the neighborhoods, he kept his eyes forward and his hands in the hoodie's pockets. When he reached his destination, he was pleased to see the head of the group standing on the steps smiling widely. These guys had been protecting Moloch's ass for years, and this time he was actually going to spend some time with them. These survivalists worshipped a form of him. They had never seen him until today, and he was in a human suit, so they were just seeing another version of him.

"Your Grace," the head guy greeted him, bowing his head. "Please come in. We have been awaiting your arrival."

Moloch nodded and walked into the house. It was very simple on the inside, white and black and full of candles. There were three other people sitting around, who immediately stood when he walked in the door. He smiled at them and followed the leader into another room.

"We have been preparing for your return," the man continued. "We procured a sacrifice, and carefully preserved her blood."

He pointed to a carafe on the table next to an over-stuffed armchair. Moloch sat down comfortably in the chair and the leader poured him a glass of blood. He sipped it and smiled, looking up at the kid.

"Tastes like a perfect 1986 aged vintage," he said in a snobby tone. "It will do, sir; it will do."

The others walked into the room and took seats on the floor in front of him, crossing their legs and staring up in awe.

Moloch liked a crowd, but this one was a bit creepy—even for him.

One by one his followers lit black candles and held them tightly in their hands. They were silent, but the mood in the house was reminiscent of the days when he had walked the Earth in his demon form and droves of followers had cast themselves at his feet to pledge their allegiance.

They had all died then, but this time it would be different. He would not let them fall.

He cleared his throat and straightened up.

"As much as I enjoy all of this, we are in a time crunch," Moloch began. "I want to start out with this: I know that when you go day after day, month after month, year after year without having your belief system verified, it can be very difficult. I am here to tell you, though, that you are *not* preparing for something that will never come. The time is here, and the time is now. You can have an apocalyptic future sooner rather than later."

"How?" the leader asked.

"By trusting me," Moloch said. "There is a group of humans on Earth who are trained warriors. They were born from our gifts, but now turn their backs on their inner demons. They are standing in the way of our complete control of that planet. I need you to give them a kick."

"How will we do that, Master?" one of the girls asked.

"You will be proactive, not waiting for the future to be handed to you," he said. "You will become my version of the Damned. You'll train and fight for liberation and freedom. We are not accepted up here, you know this, so instead of waiting for everyone else to come around, we need to take our futures into our own hands!"

"We will be more than happy to serve you," the leader declared.

"And for your service and your allegiance, when every last one of the Damned are dead and buried, you will be *rewarded.*" Moloch smiled, a deep rumbling laugh coming from his chest.

His plan was perfect, and it was working out the way he wanted.

The Damned wouldn't see this coming. They would be completely blindsided.

The days of demons being overrun, killed, and sent back to hell were over.

It was time for them to rise; for T'Chezz to lead the charge in taking Earth and all the humans on it. They would fall to their knees and grovel at his feet, thanking him and T'Chezz for being merciful and sparing their lives.

Moloch would gain his place at the left hand of Lucifer, and the humans would never cause a problem for the demons again.

The humans' time on Earth was drawing to a close. Now it was time for the Reign of the Demons.

Korbin stood in his office, looking down into the training area as Eric and Derek sparred.

He paced in his office as he had done so many times. There was a path in the carpet on the floor. where over the years he had worn away the fabric. Pacing, worrying, wondering if he was making the right decision.

He had a bad feeling in his stomach; something he had been trying to shake since he'd talked to Stephanie, but it wouldn't go away.

At first he thought that their restlessness was causing him to be restless too, but through the night his body and his instincts told him something different. There was evil in the air; more evil than normal, and even his demon— who was usually quiet—was tossing and turning inside him, warning him of something on the horizon.

He went to the workout room window and tapped on the glass, gesturing to Eric and Derek to come to his office. They nodded and grabbed their towels, drying their sweat off before disappearing out of view.

Korbin took a deep breath, not wanting to look nervous, and sat down behind his computer. He fidgeted for a moment, clasping his hands together and shifting in his seat, but finally sat still when the guys entered the office.

"What's up, boss?" Eric asked, looking alarmed. "Is there a call?"

"Not yet," Korbin replied. "As you know, Stephanie, Ella, Katie, and Charlotte are in Arizona at a retreat. Intel we received has led us to believe there is going to be an attack on the facility. The women there are all innocents. The goal of this attack is not to kill, but instead infect a large number of people. We aren't sure why, but we assume it can only be for something like an army of sorts."

"The girls have been kicking ass lately." Derek chuckled. "Katie has become a force to be reckoned with."

"She has, but she isn't invincible," Korbin replied, rubbing his chin. "I've had a bad feeling all night. I can't shake it, and I know I should listen to it."

"What do you need us to do?" Derek asked.

"I want you to go to Phoenix and find a place close to where they are staying," Korbin ordered. "I want you to be near them, but don't go in without a support request. If you go in and there is nothing going on, we may completely scare off the demons—and get the girls kicked out since it is an all-women's retreat."

"I like the sound of that." Eric chuckled.

"Keep it in your pants." Derek smirked. "They are damsels in distress."

"Or they are a bunch of Katies." Eric grinned. "Ready to kick your ass out the window."

"She can be fragile," Derek argued.

"All right, you two." Korbin waved them off. "Go. Be safe, and I'll be in contact. Let's just hope my feeling is wrong."

11

K atie knelt in front of the tables, her knees digging into the vibrantly-colored pillows beneath her. She pressed her palms together and bowed her head, peeking at the women around the tables. They were all New Age hippies and mostly her age, practicing peace while making sure not to spill anything on their designer white linen pants.

She didn't understand why they would come to a place like this if they weren't going to live the lifestyle.

In the room around them were long draping tapestries with the tree of life and several different mandalas had been embroidered on the bright purple and yellow fabrics with gold thread.

The tables were low to the ground, and there were bunches of fresh flowers all the way down the row, so a floral scent mixed with the constantly-burning incense.

Katie waited as the plates were passed around the table. The water goblets were in the center. The water pitcher had fresh fruit swirling around the bottom, which made Katie think of wine and summer. She thanked the girl next to her with a fake smile and set her plate down in front of herself.

Her stomach rumbled as she stared down at the pile of kale, scoop of quinoa, and mound of root vegetables. She was starving, but the food in front of her *still* didn't look appetizing. She glanced at Stephanie, who shrugged, picked up her fork, and pushed the food around.

Ella was already digging in, trying desperately not to roll her eyes or moan every time she took a bite. Katie knew that the food was good for her, but she had the luxury of being equipped with an anti-diet system.

Pandora would expel any of the fats and bad stuff from her body. She could literally eat anything she wanted. It was both a blessing and a curse, since Pandora was obsessed with making her tits bigger and her ass rounder— which was better than *everything* becoming bigger and rounder.

This is not what I signed up for. Pandora sighed. *I am not the least bit interested in eating something called a "root vegetable." Roots are in the ground. Let's leave them there.*

I have to admit I agree with you on this one, but I can't just slip out, Katie told her. *What if they catch me?*

Lady, you slay demons for a living. They practice something called downward-facing dog, I think you can survive a little roughing up by them. Pandora chuckled.

Katie looked at Charlotte, who was staring at her plate with one eyebrow raised. She didn't seem to be any more enthusiastic about the food then Pandora was.

Katie wanted a juicy burger, some fries, a bunch of

ketchup, a Coke, and a box of donuts for Pandora's pleasure.

She couldn't even pretend with the food she was given, especially since she couldn't think of a sweet food in the world that included a root vegetable. She sighed and leaned toward Stephanie.

"*Psst!*"

"I'm right here, Katie," she replied. "What is it?"

"I can't eat this grass." Katie pointed to her plate. "I don't think *cows* would even eat this stuff."

"What would you like me to do about that?" Stephanie asked, eyebrow raised.

"Nothing. I'm just letting you know I'm on Pandora's side on this one," Katie whispered, stopping and smiling at one of the yogis as he walked by. "I'm busting out of here. The only threat here is suicide due to excess strange vegetables...and slicing my wrists because they took away my TV."

"The only things here to slice your wrists with are the zucchini rounds," Stephanie whispered. "That might take you a bit of time."

"See? Death by fucking vegetables," Katie replied, eyeing the zucchini. "Maybe if we have to do this again I'll bring a large rabbit and hide him under my shirt. I'll feed him my food during dinner and sneak snacks in my luggage."

"Ugh, I hope we never do this again," Stephanie agreed. "I like the quiet, but *shit* I miss the guys and the ass-kickings."

"Ditto," Katie replied. "Okay, I'm serious...I'm busting the hell out of here."

Stephanie's eyes flicked around the room before she looked back to Katie. "Is this Pandora talking?"

"Not this time." Katie stood up and bowed to the girls. "See you in about five boxes of donuts."

"Hey! Bring me one," Charlotte whispered. "Help a girl the fuck out."

"You got it, sister." Katie fist-bumped with her.

Katie slipped out of the dining room, down the hall, and into her room. She sighed when she closed the door, slipping off the shawl she had been given to wear and sliding on her maroon hoodie. She grabbed her phone and a credit card and tiptoed to the bedroom door, peeking out but quickly closing it when she noticed a big group of the staff talking in the hallway.

"Shit!" Katie said. *"Shit, shit, shit."*

When she again opened the door and peered out, one of the staff noticed her. She shut the door again and cursed, gritting her teeth. She had come this far. There was no way she was going to fail at this point. She was going to get the donuts, and she was going to rub them all over her body.

That is disgusting, Pandora grumbled. *Let's stick with eating them—unless you mean doing that and having a guy lick the sugar off? Yum! That sounds delicious!*

I was joking. Katie sighed.

I'm not joking that you better find a way out of here before I start throwing things and bring you a whole lot of attention, Pandora threatened.

I'm going, I'm going. Sheesh, Katie threw her hands in the air.

She looked around her room. She was on the bottom

floor, but none of the windows opened very far. They were cranking kind, not ones that slid up and down.

She was about to give up when she remembered the room had a balcony or patio thing. She crept into the other room and opened the patio door, nonchalantly walking out as if she were just taking the air. When she didn't see anyone around, she shoved her phone and card in her pocket and snuck over the railing into the garden.

She walked along with her hands behind her back, pretending to look at the flowers until the woman in the window doing dishes had gone away.

Quickly she ran over to the tall hedges that lined the property. She pulled the branches apart and sighed, realizing she was going to have to crawl underneath to get through.

She pushed through on her hands and knees, squealing as a branch snapped back and got her in the face. She cussed at it, stopping for a moment to rub her eye.

If I go blind, you are going to have to deal with it, Katie growled.

Oh, stop being so dramatic. Pandora laughed. *You looked like a complete moron sliding through the bushes like you are escaping from the mental institution.*

Maybe this is *a mental institution,* Katie mused. *Maybe they are just posing as meditation and yoga specialists so there won't be an uprising by fine citizens like me.*

Technically you aren't a citizen. You're dead, Pandora pointed out.

Oh, great. While I am crawling through the bushes to make my way off the fucking reservation of fucking idiots to get YOU donuts, you point out my death, like it wasn't traumatic enough, Katie whined.

It was fake, Pandora replied in a snarky tone. *How traumatic can a fake death be?*

Not the point. Katie finally crawled out the other side and stood up, pulling the leaves from her hair. *Ha! I made it.*

Hold on. Pandora sniffed. *We have company.*

Where? Who? Katie reached for the knife under her shirt but didn't pull it out quite yet.

About a half a mile away. Some demon, some human, Pandora told her.

Katie moved another hundred yards to hide behind a large tree near the path and waited for the group to come along.

She stood there quietly feeling nervous, but wanting to see if she could hear anything before calling Korbin. Finally the group came close enough, and she heard them talking about fifteen yards away. She could hear everything but see nothing.

"Okay, here is the deal. We need new acolytes, but we aren't killing these women," the leader of the operation hissed. "This could be a flagship attack. In order to secure our place in this race we must turn the demons loose, possess these ladies, and change their families. Then in ten years, they will come back and turn the next generation of humans. They will spread the word, and continue to do so all over the country. We will secure the demons' place among the humans."

"What if the police come?" a deeper voice asked.

"We will get as many as we can possessed by that point, then bolt," the first speaker answered. "They will lay the blame on the spa owners, and we will be in the clear. We all have alibis, and none in our party have any connection to this place. There is no reason for them to suspect us."

Katie, freaking out slightly, waited for them to pass her and circled around the tree before pulling out her phone. There was no way that the three of them could hold off all these demons and protect Charlotte at the same time.

"Dammit!" They should have brought back-up, but they hadn't and now they had to make do.

She dialed Stephanie's number and tapped her foot as she waited for her to answer.

"What is it?" Stephanie whispered. "It's nightly silent time."

"Emergency!" Katie blurted.

"What? They didn't have the crème-filled?" Stephanie cursed quietly in sympathy.

Bwahahahahahaha! I like how this girl thinks.

"No. I mean, I don't know, but that's not what I am calling about," Katie answered.

Shut up, Pandora!

Katie continued, "The demons are here. They have a crew, and they are planning on possessing all of the women, or as many as possible. It's some sick way they think they can keep their race here on this plane."

"How far away?"

"They just walked past me, so it will be any time now," Katie whispered, looking around her area. "I'm going to call Korbin and give him the skinny; see if there are any redshirts nearby who can help. I'll be right back in, but Stephanie...keep Charlotte safe. She's not a fighter, and I don't want her to get possessed."

"Got it," Stephanie answered. "See you in a minute."

Katie pressed End and stared at the bright full moon overhead.

Doom dropped into the pit of her stomach, and she wondered how she had missed that feeling all night long. She shook the thought from her mind and speed-dialed Korbin.

Stephanie turned to Ella and nodded, letting her know the attack was imminent. Ella looked at all the innocent faces around her and slowly put down her fork. Stephanie glanced at Charlotte, who for the first time looked scared.

"Listen to me," Stephanie whispered. "Get up slowly, excuse yourself, and hide out in our room. I want you in a closet, a box—whatever you can fit yourself in—out of the line of sight. I promised to keep you safe. Do you understand?"

Charlotte nodded and looked at the yogi, who was lost in meditation. Carefully she stood up and tiptoed through the pillows and out the door. Stephanie could see her start to run when she reached the hallway, and she let out a sigh of relief.

She would be safe until they could get her back out again.

There weren't enough closets in the whole place to hide the rest of these women. They needed to get them to safety without causing a mass panic, though. Stephanie had never been good at doing things without causing panic.

She really wished that Katie would get back, because she was at a loss for what to do next.

She looked at Ella and gestured to indicate that she too was leaving to get her weapons. Slowly the two girls stood and tiptoed through the group, making it out to the hallway and closing the doors behind them. They walked quickly toward their room, their bare feet slapping the marble floors.

"Katie's calling Korbin," Stephanie explained. "The demons are here, and they plan on possessing every one of those women out there."

"Why?"

"Survival, numbers, security," Stephanie listed. "Katie will be back inside in a minute, but right now the two of us need to prepare. We need our weapons, and we need a game strategy. I'm not sure if we will have help; it might just be the three of us."

"What about Charlotte?" Ella asked. "Is she a fighter?"

"No." Stephanie chuckled. "She is an underground reporter-turned-spy for our side. She has never trained a day in her life, and she is not infected. I would like to keep it that way; give that girl the chance you didn't have, Katie didn't have, and most everyone on the teams wasn't given."

"All right," Ella agreed. "We will keep her safe. Not a problem."

"As for the rest, I don't really know. We are going to have to play it by ear."

"Okay," Ella replied. "Keep Charlotte safe and kick major fucking demon ass. I think I can handle both of those things."

"Good." Stephanie smiled. "Because we are gonna have one hell of a fight on our hands."

"What's good?" Korbin answered.

"At the moment? Nothing," Katie replied.

"What's going on?" he demanded, immediately dropping the playful tone.

"The demons are here. It's going down. Warn the locals; that is very important in case one of these motherfuckers escape. And by one, I am saying there are a lot of them. There isn't any chance that there are redshirts in the area are there?"

"I'll go you one better," Korbin told her. "I sent Derek and Eric to stay close by in case this very thing happened. I'll dispatch them to you."

"Perfect." Katie sighed. "You are always on top of things."

"I had a hunch," he explained. "Be careful, and call me when it's over. Oh, and please protect Charlotte."

"Already on it." Katie headed back toward the house.

1 2

Stephanie laid her weapons out on the bed as Ella dropped her shawl and pulled her vest over her shoulders, zipping it up in the front. She grabbed her swords and slid them into the back sheaths, then glanced at Charlotte. The woman looked terrified, so she sighed and rubbed Charlotte's back.

"You are going to be just fine, and if all else fails, kick them in the balls," Ella explained.

"That is my new motto," Stephanie replied. "If all else fails, kick 'em in the balls."

Just then the door flew open and all three girls jumped back. Stephanie grabbed her chest and breathed heavily as she stared at Katie.

"Do you always have to be so dramatic?" Stephanie asked. "The door was unlocked; a simple twist of the handle would have sufficed."

"Yeah but then I couldn't laugh at your terrified little

faces." Katie stuck out her tongue. "All right, we gotta get moving. We gotta get these women into their rooms."

"Okay, Charlotte." Ella nodded. "Get in the closet, and don't come out until I come back to get you. You are going to be fine. What's the rule?"

"If all else fails, kick 'em in the balls," she whimpered.

"Hmmm." Katie rubbed her chin. "I fucking *love* that rule."

"I know, right?" Stephanie smiled. "Too bad I already claimed it."

"Meh, you can't stop these lips from spilling those words." Katie smiled and hip-checked her. "All right, ladies, you ready? Oh, and fear not…Eric and Derek will be joining us soon."

"Oh, swoon." Stephanie looked at her. "I think we got this."

"Maybe," Katie replied.

The three girls sprinted out the door, Ella taking a moment to shut and lock the door behind them. They sped down the marble hallways, still barefoot, their feet slapping against the cold stone. They swung open the dining room doors, causing the patrons to gasp and cry out. Stephanie jumped onto the table as Katie and Ella walked toward the back, scanning everyone, to make sure there were no red eyes in the crowd.

"There is an emergency," Stephanie yelled as she raised her arms in the air. "I need everyone including staff to stand up and calmly go to your rooms. Once there, lock the doors and don't open for anyone unless you hear us over the loudspeaker first. This is not a drill, this is the real deal. Your lives are in danger."

Stephanie dropped her arms and watched the women gab nervously to each other. For a moment she thought maybe she had spoken the wrong language, but then she realized these women were rich bitches who weren't used to anything being an emergency except their much-needed dye jobs.

Stephanie looked at Katie and shrugged, not knowing what to do.

"Hey!" Ella yelled. "Did you guys hear her?"

Still nothing. They were completely unable to understand that they needed to get the hell up and hide before bloodsucking demons came and took their souls.

Remember...if they get infected, they will probably eat more grass and you won't have to.

Don't tempt me, Pandora.

That is kind of my middle name. You breathe, I tempt.

Katie put her hands on her hips, double-checking that she really needed to help these women.

She remembered her responsibilities and sighed.

"Hey," a voice came from behind Stephanie. "Get your asses up!"

A smiling Charlotte, wearing a vest and carrying a knife, stepped around Stephanie.

"I can't be scared forever, right?" she asked.

"Whoop!" Ella raised a fist. "Charlotte's here to kick some ass."

All the women started to get to their feet, but none were leaving the room. Katie rolled her eyes and looked around for a fire alarm or something.

Instead, her eyes fell on a beautiful ice sculpture of a

woman surrounded by grasses and flowers. She grabbed her pistol from its holster and pointed it at the ice.

She pulled the trigger and blew the thing to pieces. Ice went flying everywhere and all of the women screamed, ducking and staring at her.

"THIS IS NOT A DRILL! Now that I have your attention," she waved her pistol toward the exits, "I need everyone to hurry. Run to your rooms and lock the doors."

She put her gun in the air and raised her eyebrows. The women took off down the hallways to lock themselves in their rooms. Katie holstered her gun, brushing her hands together.

Stephanie watched them leave. "And *that* is how you get the damn thing done, Mama."

"These women are fucking impossible." Katie shook her head. "Charlotte, are you sure you want to do this? You don't have any experience."

"I'm sure," she replied emphatically.

"All right, take my gun." Katie handed her one of her two pistols. "Just point it at the demon's head and *BLAM*!"

Ella nodded her head. "Works every time."

Just then they heard a noise from outside.

The demons had arrived.

Ella went over to the window and peered into the small canyon at the edge of the property. It was dark, but red eyes reflected at her.

"That is a whole lot of fucking red eyes," Ella commented from beside her, a touch of concern in her voice.

"Let me see," Stephanie exclaimed, excitedly running across the tables and jumping down to look out the window. "Wow, they really brought the show today. They are here for the fucking win."

"No matter how many of them there are, we have something they don't," Katie stated.

"Wheatgrass?" Ella asked.

"No," Katie ground out. "Souls."

"Come on, let's show them what Korbin's Killers are made of." Stephanie checked her weapons. "Then we'll get some fucking donuts."

I like that girl more every day, Pandora declared.

Stephanie led the group as they headed outside. She was giddy; excited to show those bastards a good time.

A *very* good time. Well, at least for her.

"Oh, shit. That's a lot." She stopped to reassess as the numbers caught up, then shrugged. She was there to kick ass and not take names, and that was exactly what she was going to do.

The four girls lined up and looked down at the possessed, who were surprised to see defenders.

Stephanie twirled her knife in her hand.

She looked at Katie and flashed her a huge smile.

If she is feeling fear, she hides it well, Pandora commented. *She could do with a little fear. Fear helps the body sense threats.*

Katie nodded as Stephanie let out a battle cry that echoed across the grounds.

With that she sprinted into the group, slashing her knife from side to side. The feeling of warm blood on her hands did something to her, and her eyes flashed bright red.

"Come here, demon babies. I got your soul right here," Stephanie called, jumping onto a demon's shoulders and twisting his head to snap his neck.

"That's going to leave a mark!" Ella called.

Stephanie jumped down before his body even collapsed and moved on to the next.

The demons snarled and growled, backing up as Katie, Ella, and Charlotte entered the fray on both sides of Stephanie.

Stephanie had sprays of blood on her face and she laughed as she ran forward, her short sword high in the air. She swiped low, taking two demons out at the knees and jabbing her sword into their chests.

She pulled the sword out with a grunt and wiped the black blood from her face, slightly disgusted by the taste of blood on her lips.

She raised her fingers to her nose and breathed deeply as she felt the adrenaline rolling through her. She was angry—*very* angry—and she wasn't going to let those bastards win, no matter how many of them there were.

She rolled across the ground and sprang to her feet, turning away just as a demon swiped across her arm. She gasped and clenched her teeth totally pissed at what had just happened.

"You cut my fifty-dollar motherfucking hippy shirt, you bitch," she growled at the female human standing there. Stephanie smiled, tossing her knife in the air. "Time to go night-night, little girl."

She lunged forward to cold-cock the girl and she went

down like a fucking sack of potatoes. Stephanie laughed and stepped over the girl, determined not to kill any humans but definitely not letting them get away with that shit. She looked around and sighed; more demons were coming at them from the sides.

"There are a lot of these fuckers!" she yelled. "Workout time!!!"

Katie laughed as Stephanie went pure postal on demons and humans alike, then ran up behind her teammate and grabbed a demon by the ear, dragging him away. She flipped him around by pulling on his ear and shook her finger in his face.

"Sneaking up on a girl is not very nice," Katie told him. She pulled her knife out of its sheath and tossed it in the air. "And what do we do with not-nice demons?"

Katie rolled her neck, opened her mouth, and yelled with her and Pandora's combined voice.

"We fucking kill them!"

She caught the knife by the handle and plunged it deep into the demon's chest. The demon screamed in horror before bursting into ash. Katie smiled, still holding her knife.

Behind you.

Turning quickly, Katie kicked another demon in the chest.

He flew backward, knocking down several others like dominoes. Katie shook her head at the stupidity and ran straight for the group, diving into them and wrestling one to the ground. She sliced her knife across his chest and he screamed as she plunged it into his heart. He crumbled to ash beneath her and she stood up, brushing off the dust.

She was getting a workout. Dodge one demon, kick at another. Evade the counter and stab a third. Every time a demon ran toward her she had to block or evade, and occasionally stab at their weak points. With Pandora she was beating ass, but it was tough. They were being overrun.

Help would hopefully get there fast.

Ella was overwhelmed by the sheer number of demons who had shown up for the party.

Normally she would fight two or three demons, but this was an all-out war. They just kept coming. She took a deep breath and ran screaming into a new group, her swords slashing.

She mowed through a group of demons like she was cutting through vines in the jungle. Their screams echoed around her, but she liked it. She *wanted* it, and she could taste the bloodthirst on her lips.

Use martial arts, Melneck urged. *I'll help.*

Ella, out of breath, nodded and sheathed her swords. Immediately she started a kata, flowing from one move to another.

With every punch and kick, Melneck increased her power tenfold. Her fist hit the side of a demon's head and knocked it clean off his shoulders. As she followed the blow through a demon's claw caught her on the collarbone and ripped the skin open. She snarled at him and he smirked at her.

"You motherfucker, that was where my next tattoo was going!" She punched him in the nose and watched the surprise on his face as the blood shot out. "Now I gotta pick a new spot, because nobody wants a tattoo over a fresh wound."

"I. Don't!" She punched him.

"Think." She punched him again.

"That shit is funny!" She punched him over and over, following him as he stumbled backward. He held his nose as blood rolled down his face.

When she'd had enough, she punched him as hard as she could, knocking him to the ground, and he came to a stop at Stephanie's feet. Stephanie smiled and swung her sword, slicing his face in half.

Ella shrugged and turned back to the fight. "I always liked Two-Face in the comic books."

There were so many.

"I couldn't have picked some other night to face my fears?" Charlotte groaned as she looked at all the demons.

The other girls were putting a dent in the enemy, but they continued to arrive from somewhere.

A female demon, her teeth sharp and her red eyes wild, ran straight at Charlotte. There were scars across her face as if she had been slashed.

"Dammit!" She raised her pistol. "Time to learn how to shoot."

She aimed at the woman, closing one eye and squinting the other. She let out a deep breath and pulled the trigger, and a hole formed between the demon's eyes as brain matter and blood sprayed out the back of her head. Her body, dead before it hit the ground, flew backward to land on some decorative rocks.

Charlotte shook as she glanced around. They *looked* like humans, but she knew deep inside that whatever was human was already gone.

"I didn't kill a human, it was a demon. I didn't kill a human..." She kept the mantra going.

The humans had left their shell for the demon to use.

Charlotte aimed away from the other girls and just started spraying bullets into the crowd of demons. She managed to shoot three, including the one who had come at her. She liked fighting the bastards; tonight had completely changed everything.

She had wanted to see the demons get their justice.

Now she didn't give a shit anymore. It might have been the adrenaline or it could have been frustration from years of seeing the results, but tonight, at least, she was making a dent.

She was part of the battle for humanity, and that was good enough for her.

―――――――――

The girls cleared the area and stepped back against the fence, wiping the blood from their faces as they gazed around.

They breathed deeply, exhausted.

Slowly they all looked up; nine more demons, snarling and growling down at them, lined the roof edge just one floor above the dining room window.

Katie pulled out a sword and crouched, and the other girls followed her actions. "Don't suppose they would choke on that fucking lemongrass?"

"Dammit, I'm out of bullets here, folks," Charlotte complained. "Not to sound like a whiner, but can I get another clip or magazine or doohickey full of bullets to shove up the ass of this pistol?"

Ella snickered as Katie handed her a magazine. "It's the handle."

"Ass, butt, handle...take this enema, you metallic sonofabitch," Charlotte griped. "My hands sting already."

Before they could move, though, shots rang out and the demons fell over the edge to land in the bushes under the window.

There were a few screams from inside the building.

"You girls didn't leave anything for us," Eric griped, joining them and looking at the demons.

"You were slow." Stephanie shrugged as she pointed to the piles of ash. "Early bird catches the worm."

The guys helped them tend their wounds.

Katie's were basically healed, and Stephanie's weren't really bad. Eric put some stitches in Ella as she winced. Charlotte watched Eric work.

"You did good." Eric opened his case and grabbed a bandage before turning back to Ella. "I saw you fighting."

"Yeah." She winced a bit when he pulled the stitches closed. "But I need to do a hell of a lot better. Just wait... next time I'll be just like *them*."

Eric, Derek, Charlotte, and Ella looked at Stephanie and Katie, who were standing at the edge of the grassy area as the sun began to peak over the horizon.

"Feel like a hero?" Katie asked Stephanie as orange light outlined the mountains in the distance.

"Kinda?" Stephanie answered.

"How about being a badass chick?"

"Yeah." Stephanie nodded. "I like that quite a bit."

13

Charlotte, Katie, Stephanie, and Ella were more than happy to bring their battered and bruised asses back to Vegas.

Even Eric and Derek were glad they didn't have to participate in another fight like that for a while. At least they hoped it would be a while.

Katie and Charlotte took the chopper back from Arizona, and the rest of the team flew back on the jet. They arrived shortly after the jet landed and choppered everyone back to the base. Ella chose to go with them, since the plane was going to need a little maintenance before it took her home.

When they landed at the new base Damian, Korbin, and Calvin were waiting outside for them.

Katie sighed, knowing she was going to have to explain the women who were claiming she shot at them, but at the point when no one would move she really hadn't cared about the repercussions.

They got out of the helicopter and stretched, then made their way over to the tent in the center of the grounds.

"Welcome back." Korbin smiled. "I'm glad you're in one piece. I heard it was a hell of a fight."

"I hurt in places I didn't think I could hurt." Ella rubbed her shoulder and smiled at Calvin. "Hey, buddy."

"Hey there." He grinned. "Girls sure did show you a good time, didn't they?"

"Don't we always?" Stephanie answered and patted Calvin on the shoulder as she walked past him. "Never a dull day in our world."

"That's for sure." Katie chuckled as she threw her bag over her shoulder. "I'm hungry. We got anything to eat in this new joint?"

"There's food inside." Korbin smiled. "We pretty much have the whole place set up to stay here now."

"Good," Katie said. "I could use a shower and a cup of tea. How about you, Charlotte? You want some tea?"

"Why not? I got no place to rush off to," she agreed, catching up with Katie.

"Welcome to your second home," Katie replied, putting her arm around Charlotte. "You handled yourself well, and that is a gold star in my book."

"Wait…" Korbin called after them, his eyes narrowed. "You did *what*? I thought you were hiding in a closet?"

The girls kept straight faces and rushed toward the doors.

"Hey," Korbin yelled. "Wait!"

He stomped after them.

"Lord." Stephanie sighed. She was standing with Calvin, Derek, Eric, Damian, and Ella. "I guess I should go help put out the fire on that one. Ella, it was a pleasure, as always."

"Whelp." Derek sighed, watching Stephanie walk toward the building. "I am about to go play with my gadgets, but it was a real pleasure working with you, Ella. You did well out there. Have fun in New York."

"Stay alive, my friend," she ordered, leaning in and giving him a hug.

He nodded at the others and headed toward the IT entrance. Ella put her arms up in the air and stretched, yawning loudly.

"Well, I guess I should be heading back," Ella said, looking at the pilot who was waiting in the helicopter.

Calvin took out his tablet and hit the Send button on a message. "Yeah, we're just waiting for the plane to refuel, and we can get on our way."

Ella eyed him. "Uh, I am grown, and I fight demons, I don't think I need a chaperone."

"Good, cause I'm not one," Calvin replied. "I am just doing the honors since you helped our team. Korbin likes to know his people are taken care of, get home safely, and are happy."

"'Cause I'm a girl." She rolled her eyes.

"That's my cue." Eric turned to walk away, waving a hand over his shoulder. "Have a safe trip back, Ella!" Damian followed him toward the building.

"Thanks." Ella smiled as she waved at them.

"Not because you are a woman," Calvin explained. "Because you are *important*."

"So who's riding back with *you*?" Ella asked raising her eyebrows. "I mean, you're important to Korbin."

"He knows I can handle anything or anyone," Calvin told her, heading toward the chopper.

"Oh, because demon attacks on a jet in midair happen so often." She smirked. "Sure, I can see it. One minute you're relaxing in your chair and the next minute a demon is popping out of the air vent trying to wrestle your soul to hell."

"Come on, trouble," he directed, opening the chopper's door and pointing inside.

"Okay." She paused in the doorway with a sly smile. "Let me ask you this: are you in the mile-high club? Cause I hear that ninety-eight percent of black men—"

"*Get in the chopper,*" he ordered, staring at her.

"That's what I thought." She smiled as she sat down. "The rumors are true!"

After they finished talking to Korbin, Katie silently followed Stephanie down the corridors that sloped down to the main living quarters.

Katie hadn't been in her new room yet, but they would have made it comfortable for her.

She wasn't really the type to complain, and she knew she could change things around if she wanted. Katie wasn't sure she would see the old base again. It was all for the best, though. She had never been good with goodbyes, especially when they were inanimate objects like a house or room. She glanced at Stephanie, who was smiling.

"Why do you look so happy?"

"I just think it was amazing how quickly I got Korbin to

drop his attack on us for letting Charlotte fight." She giggled. "Though I'm sure she is getting a good lecture right now."

"You do have a way with Korbin," she agreed, stopping as they passed a window just above ground-level.

Katie went up on her tiptoes to peer out. Sand blew wildly through the air, and the fence swayed slightly with the wind. Stephanie smiled and waited for her.

"They finished the giant chain link fence with razor wire," Katie said. "Things are definitely coming along."

"That they are." Stephanie nodded and opened the door leading to the main area.

I don't think a chain link fence and a little razor wire is going to keep demons out, Pandora snorted.

It's not for the demons, it's for the idiot humans so they know not to trespass, Katie explained. *Once you cross it you get blown to bits, and I really don't want chunks of little Johnny in my morning coffee.*

Oh, castle-style fortifications... How quaint, Pandora exclaimed. *Though I'm not really sure if any of that would help much against T'Chezz.*

The next morning, Katie was more than happy to get out of her new bed and spring into action.

She had definitely slept better on a mattress that wasn't a hundred years old and didn't have springs that beat into her spine all night long.

She knew Korbin had replaced their mattresses on purpose; if the team slept well, they would be more apt to work out in the new training center. Why she hadn't complained at the old base when that one damned spring had started to annoy her, she wasn't sure.

It wasn't like she couldn't have just purchased a new mattress and had it delivered.

She left her room dressed and ready and headed down the corridor to the training center, which was about a five-minute walk and on the left. She felt like she was living in a submarine, but in a lot of ways she liked it.

As soon as she stepped in she squinted from the sunlight shining through the ceiling, which was tinted glass. and when you looked up, you could see the sand blowing across it. If you were walking around outside you wouldn't even see it until you were right on it. It was a pretty cool idea, most likely born from Stephanie's brain.

Katie took a lap around the track to warm up and grabbed her quarterstaff, gripping it tightly and moving it in sharp, thoughtful motions. She had been practicing with it for a while and had actually gotten pretty good with it. Eric and Derek came over to her and motioned to the floor.

"You wanna spar with us?" Eric asked.

"What, both of you?"

"Yep." Derek smirked. "Unless we're too much for you."

"Right." Katie laughed. "Get your asses out there. Let's see what you two idiots are made of."

Katie and the guys entered the ring, and Derek took several playful swipes at her. Katie smiled charmingly and waited for him to stand up before slashing her staff at his ankles, which knocked him to the ground. She quickly moved over him and thrust her staff toward his face, stopping just an inch from his nose. He put his hands up and laughed as Katie pulled it back and helped him to his feet.

"So we are playing rough." Derek smiled. "Noted."

"Hey!" Stephanie called as she walked into the training center. "What are you idiots doing?"

"Testing Katie's new skills." Eric was in a defensive position.

"Oh, I gotta get in on this." Stephanie laughed and tossed her bag to the side. "You think you can take the three of us?"

"*Pfft.*" Katie rolled her eyes. "Please, fighting you three would be like one tiny demon. Bring it on."

Stephanie immediately ran forward and attacked, knocking Katie off balance. She caught her footing and swung her staff at Eric, who dodged it as he attempted to sneak up on her. The three threw punches innocently at first, but really got into it once Katie swiped her stick across Stephanie's arm.

"You want to do this thing huh?" Stephanie laughed. "All right, I got you."

Katie defended herself pretty well at first, but her human strength faded. She was panting after about ten minutes of fighting all three of them off, and the stick got heavier in her hands the longer they sparred. Derek feinted at her, bringing her attention to him while Stephanie and Eric snuck to her sides and attacked simultaneously. They brought their arms around her chest and took her to the floor, pinning her. Derek laughed as she laid there catching her breath.

"*Okay, enough of this shit,*" Pandora growled, juicing Katie's energy. "*Kick their asses.*"

Katie's breathing went back to normal and she kicked her feet into the air and bounced up, tossing Eric and Stephanie to the side. She twirled the staff around her and stopped with it in front of her body. All three of her team-mates were now in defensive poses, pausing for only a second before lunging at her. With two swipes she took all three of them down, chuckling as they fell to the floor. She raised her staff to vertical, bowed, and walked off the mat, leaving them on the ground bitching in pain.

Stephanie laid on her back on the mat, trying to focus. The ceiling came into view and she looked at the sun through the heavily tinted glass. She picked up her head, but let it fall back to the floor with a groan.

"What just happened?" she whimpered, looking to the side as a shadow approached her.

"It looks like you got your ass handed to you," Korbin told her, leaning over her. "Katie's demon decided she'd had enough of you guys beating on Katie, and I guess she decided to join in. Don't worry, you aren't the first and won't be the last to be bested by her inner growl. I personally think it's an important lesson for you."

Stephanie groaned again and closed her eyes, both her head and her legs throbbing.

She had never been bested, but that was before. She suddenly had more of an appreciation for what Katie could do.

Apparently she'd been holding back on their missions, not letting her demon take too much control. With her demon juicing her she could take down an entire army and not even blink an eye.

Stephanie's demon didn't do very much. She had to rely

on the skills she had learned growing up with a group of people who all felt they needed to know how to protect themselves. She was starting to think that with demons like the ones she saw the day before and Damned like Katie walking around, they might not have been so wrong.

Their training had been horrible, but at least they knew how to protect themselves.

She pushed herself up on her elbows and looked at Derek and Eric, who were struggling to pick themselves up from the floor. When she'd said she could take them all, she hadn't been kidding. Stephanie pulled up her pant leg and looked at the bruise that was already forming.

"Great," she mumbled.

"Come on." Korbin laughed, reaching down and helping her to her feet.

She stood up and grabbed his shoulder for support as she wobbled back and forth. She felt the pain where the staff had hit her hard. Stephanie shook her head, rolled her eyes, and looked at Korbin.

"And what lesson are you talking about?" she asked. "To stay away from wooden sticks?"

"No." He chuckled as he walked off the mat. "Years of practice don't make up for millennia of preparation."

"For her demon." Stephanie scoffed to herself.

She hobbled off the mat and sat down on a bench, rubbing her leg. She glanced at Katie as Korbin passed her, giving her a high five.

Stephanie laughed, shaking her head and grabbing her bag. She had started out her day's training with an ass-kicking, which only made her want to work harder.

Stephanie put her iPod's earbuds in and cranked up the

tunes, then put her lifting gloves on. She winced when she stood up and laughed at herself. The bruise would be a good reminder to stay on top of her game. She didn't have the bounce-back that twenty-somethings did—not that she was old.

She started to load the new deadlift bar with weights. Eric, who had been rejuvenated by the fight and was bouncing up and down, joined her. He chugged some water and smiled.

"You need some help with those, little lady?" He laughed.

"Only if you want to find one of them lodged in your asshole," she growled.

"Whoa there." He chuckled and put his hands up. "Carry on, please. Get some of that aggression out."

Stephanie was aware that she was showing aggression, but as she watched Korbin disappear down the hallway she remembered exactly what she was stressed about. It wasn't the demons, and she didn't have a problem being shown up by Katie.

She knew exactly what kind of activity would relieve her stress. She sighed and went back to the weights. That was way far off.

14

K atie laughed as she put up her staff and grabbed her boots, sitting down and lacing them up as she watched Korbin help Stephanie up off the mat.

Part of her felt bad, but mostly she just felt proud that she had been able to take down three of her teammates in seconds—thanks to Pandora of course. When she was done she walked toward the door, stopping as Korbin walked past. He put up his hand and gave her a high five, winking at her before walking down the hall.

She smiled at Stephanie and left the training area, heading to the elevator. She squinted hard as it breached the surface and slid its heavy metal doors open.

She put up her hand to block the sun as she made her way to Joshua's building, which she hadn't had the chance to check out yet. When she went inside she was impressed; he had decorated the place and added furniture. It pretty much looked like the inside of Wayne Manor, except it was one very large open room.

Joshua was in the back corner, his goggles over his eyes as he hammered some metal. When he was done he looked up and smiled, pushing his goggles up and standing up with the weapon. He quenched it in a nearby tub of water and placed it on the table behind him.

"Hey there, buddy." Katie smiled. "Am I interrupting?"

"Nope." he smiled. "I was actually hoping you would come see me today."

On his way over to her, he stopped at a large cabinet and opened a drawer, pulling out three plastic boxes. The boxes held rounds, a hundred in each. Katie ran her hand over the tips, feeling the magic inside them.

"That's three hundred," he told her proudly. "I hoped to have more, but these are ready to test."

"How do they work?" she demanded.

"Well, as they enter the body the bullet mushrooms, ejecting the harmful metal. That is when it causes problems. They'll kill just like any other bullet, but I know how hard head shots are to make during a fight. These will disable most demons with one shot anywhere in the body so you can chop their head off or burn em' or whatever you find necessary. Multiple hits should work on the big ones, but you have to aim really well to get the best result."

"Nice," Katie replied. "So if I can shoot him between the eyes use a regular bullet."

"If you want to save the rounds, yes." Joshua smiled. "Those are yours, of course."

"Awesome! Thank you." Katie accepted the three yellow plastic boxes. "Hey, I have a question."

"Shoot."

"I was wondering if you would take a look at my quarterstaff. I want to see if it can be modified to have extendable blades. The end cap would be made of our metal, and I want to be able to remove the blades. I know it sounds crazy, but I have really been working on perfecting my skills. I can't kill a demon with a wooden stick, and if I'm going to go farther I want to be able to damage or kill with it. I don't want to just add a step to my fighting, you know?"

"Yeah, you want to make the most of your energy." Joshua pursed his lips, thinking. "We can definitely do something. Come over here and let's draw it out."

Katie walked over to his drafting table and pulled up a chair, impressed with how professionally he did everything. It was definitely a change from the basement of the old building at the last base. Joshua pulled out some pencils and a piece of paper and quickly sketched out the staff as it was at that moment.

"I saw your staffs when we moved," he commented, finishing up the initial drawing. "That is what you have right now, so we'll add the tip right there. How do you want it to work?"

"I was thinking a button that unlocks the shaft," Katie explained. "From there it's manual, as in I have to twist the shaft. Once twisted, it should lock into place. I was thinking something like eighteen-inch dirks coming out either from the sides to allow a slicing motion or one that springs from the tip that can be used to stab. Either way is fine."

"Okay." Joshua nodded as he drew the end of the staff.

"Like that?"

"Yes." Katie smiled. "Just don't make it so narrow that they break off. Demon skin is thick and hard, so I don't want it to be a one-and-done kind of thing."

"Right, so it needs to be thick, and it needs to be reinforced in some way," he repeated, making notes. "I think I can come up with something relatively quickly. It'll just take me a little bit of time to forge the dirk."

"Sweet." Katie smiled. "You are doing an amazing job. I just want you to know that."

"Thanks." He blushed. "But I'm not on my own. I have a whole lot of help."

"I think that is true across the board." Katie chuckled. "We all have a lot of help in one way or another, but we are family and we do things together. If you need anything, just let me know."

"I appreciate it." As she headed toward the door he lowered his voice. "More than you know."

Derek walked out of the elevator into the bright sun, putting his hands on his hips and looking around. He squinted to stare at the sands in the distance. He wanted to do something—relax, have a good time—but he had no idea what that something was.

He didn't feel like driving to the Strip or dealing with all those people, but out here in the middle of nowhere his options were limited.

He headed over to the makeshift garage Korbin had set up.

The concrete base was new, and they had erected a large tent over it to shield the vehicles from the sand. Derek went in and stared at Katie's truck, admiring its sleek lines and ability to handle almost anything. The SUVs were great for transport, but that baby looked like she was built for fun.

"She's pretty sweet, isn't she?" Katie offered as she came up behind Derek.

"Yeah." He laughed. "Have you taken her out? You know, really given her a proper test drive?"

"Nope." Katie shrugged and tossed him the keys. "Now is as good a time as any."

"Really?" he exclaimed, looking at the keys in his hands.

She opened the passenger door. "Yep, but you break her, you fix her."

"Deal," he agreed, climbing hastily into the driver's seat before she came to her senses.

He buckled his seatbelt and started the engine, rubbing his hands on the steering wheel once she started purring. He looked at Katie and smiled as he grabbed the shifter.

"You ready?"

"Hell, yeah." Katie waved him forward. "Let's open this baby up!"

Derek tore down the road and out the main gate. As soon as he had gone far enough, he exited the road by taking a sharp right into the sand.

They flew through the desert, jumping washes, doing donuts, and laughing. He gunned it in an open area, grabbing the emergency brake and slamming on the brake pedal, whirling the car in a three-sixty and coming to a stop. Katie laughed madly as she swayed back and forth, holding onto the overhead grip.

"Okay," she said, unbuckling. "My turn."

Oh shit.

Shut up, Pandora. I haven't killed us yet.

"Yet" is the operative word here, honey.

They switched spots and took off again, exploring every part of the land around them. From a distance, you could tell exactly where they were by the dust plumes in the air.

Katie realized that she had been born to off-road in the Raptor; it just felt so right and so natural to her. She could take whatever turns she wanted and go as fast as she wanted, and when she let go of fear she had a fantastically good time.

She slowed the truck down as they approached the rocky and mountainous terrain on the back end of the massive property.

Stephanie had finally come clean on just how many acres she owned, and Katie felt like it was a damned state.

It wasn't, but that many zeroes should equal a state-sized chunk of land.

Katie shifted into four-wheel low and slowly began to climb the mountain, smiling in excitement as Derek stared at the scenery. When they finally reached a point where the mountain became too steep she stopped and parked, and they climbed a little farther to sit on a flat area cut into the mountain.

It would be perfect for sitting or lying down to watch the stars.

"Wow." she gasped as the sun dipped beyond the horizon.

The sky was orange and the clouds that had gathered right at the horizon glistened in beautiful yellows and pinks. It was a really nice moment; something she hadn't yet shared with anyone from the team.

Derek sighed and leaned back on his hands, closing his eyes and enjoying the cool breeze.

"I could definitely get used to living here." He smiled. "I've got my family, my computers, and a hell of a beautiful view. I don't think I could ask for much more."

"Maybe a pizza place that delivered out here." Katie giggled. "I'm starving."

"It's getting dark anyway." Derek smiled as he got up and swatted off the dust. "Come on, let's gun it back. There isn't anything out here that can hurt us."

"Except demons and wolves." Katie shrugged. "But fuck them."

Derek laughed heartily as they climbed back into the truck. Katie took the helm, and they slowly crept back down the mountain, not wanting to slip or flip the vehicle.

When they reached the bottom they went balls out. Katie slammed her foot on the gas, spinning the tires before diving into the sandbox in front of them. She laughed and cheered as they sped through the desert, her window down and her arm out to feel the wind blow past.

"It's getting dark," she yelled over the wind.

Pandora laughed. *You don't need lights.*

Suddenly Katie's eyes sparkled brightly, and she could see in the dark. It was like wearing night vision, only everything had a red tint—and she could see perfectly.

Derek looked at her and laughed, shaking his head.

"You've got the coolest demon. She like installs toys in your body," he commented. "Night-vision Katie. Maybe I can con my demon into x-ray vision."

"Pervert." Katie pulled hard to the right to avoid a large rock.

Katie gunned it and hit a slope, going airborne for a moment before landing and throwing sand behind them. The wheels caught, and they took off, swerving back and forth watching as the front gate came into view. She slowed the truck just a bit and took the turn through the gate at high speed, tilting the truck almost on two wheels. Derek clung to the oh-shit handle as they leveled out, causing Katie to erupt in laughter.

"How did he die?" Derek said. "Oh, he went four-wheeling with a demon and ended up inside a giant ball of metal."

"Ha! That was what that last demon said." Katie laughed, thinking about the Ferrari.

They sped up the driveway, slowing down only to pull into the garage. She put the truck in park and turned off the engine, leaning her head back as she continued to laugh. When the giggling simmered down, she turned her head and looked at Derek. He looked more alive than she had ever seen him before.

"This was fun." She grinned.

"Hell, yeah it was." He nodded vigorously. "I was seriously expecting us to crash any second. I pictured taking one of those peaks and just rolling end over end through the sand."

"That would have been a shame." Katie paused for a

moment. "I think I would stop buying cars if that had happened."

They sat there for a minute looking out the front window before both turning and speaking in unison.

"Yeah right!"

Derek pointed to her. "Seriously, I can see you owning like fifteen cars during your reign as Damned Queen."

"Damned what?"

"Oh, that's just what we call you: the Damned Queen." Derek smiled. "You can kick anyone and anything's ass."

"Not anything." She sighed and opened the car door.

"One day it *will* be anything." Derek stood on the running board and looked over the truck bed at her. "You will get there. Just you watch and see."

"And when I do, we will all be out of a job." Katie closed the door.

"Nah. As long as there is a Satan we will have a job," he assured her as they walked toward the building.

Lucifer.

"Then I guess I have bigger fish to fry."

"That would be the ultimate bad-guy showdown." He chuckled and mimicked putting a microphone up to his mouth. "Katie versus Lucifer, LIVE at Wrigley Field!"

"Wrigley?" she laughed.

"I don't know. It was the first thing that came to mind. I like baseball," he admitted.

They walked into the building and took the elevator down to the passages below. As they stepped off, Katie looked toward Korbin's office.

"See you later tonight for soaps?" Derek asked.

"You got it, dude." Katie waved. "I'm gonna just go talk to Korbin for a few. I'll meet you up there."

"Perfect," he said as he walked away.

"Hey there." Korbin looked up as he filed the last of his paperwork. "What can I do for you, Katie?"

"I was wondering something," she replied, strolling in and examining his new digs. "I was wondering if I could speak to the general?"

"Uh, why?" Korbin asked, frowning. "You changing teams?"

"God, no." Katie shook her head vehemently. "I just think that he is a good enough man to owe me a favor, after what we did the last time we worked with him. I'd like to get ahead of him on some things. Plus, I'm going to give him a hundred rounds of the new 9mm bullets Joshua made."

"Katie, I don't think—" Korbin started, but she put up a hand.

"No, you *aren't* thinking. I need to be proactive. You guys are all strutting around like peacocks trying to show each other up. It's a dick-measuring contest, and I don't want to be part of that. I think he needs something from our side, and if I offer it he is less likely to just take it."

"Ugh," Korbin replied, rubbing his face. "You sure you want to get mixed up in the politics?"

"Hell no, but it's what's best." Katie shrugged.

"All right." He sighed. "I mean, it's your company, boss.

But I'm warning you now: you need to be careful. These guys don't give two shits; they will screw us in a heartbeat."

"I hear you, and appreciate the warning." Katie stood up. "Thanks, Boss Number Two."

Korbin scowled as Katie giggled and left the room.

15

K atie felt good after her conversation with Korbin.

She might be able to step in and create a more peaceful relationship between the mercenaries and the military. She didn't want the mercs and military to work together at the moment—*that* had been a disaster—but Katie wanted to keep the peace so she could keep her business intact.

Katie's mother had always told her to keep her friends close and her enemies closer. They weren't necessarily the enemy, but they could easily become one very fast.

She went into her room and turned on the shower to warm up, then stripped down and hopped in.

The new showers had huge shower heads, creating a waterfall effect. It was so much better than the old ones, which had barely sprayed consistently in one direction.

She was just glad to not have to clean up puddles after showering; the doors definitely helped. As she stood there washing her hair and looking at her loofa, she realized something.

Uh, Pandora, Katie began.

Yes, my dear? she replied sarcastically.

I don't think I've had to shave in about four months. Like the razor still has the plastic guard on it.

I know, she chirped. *I figured it was one of those things you really didn't need to waste your time on, so I stopped the growth.*

Even, um, down there?

Especially down there, Pandora grumbled. *This is not a garden, no matter what people say. We are not just going to just let it grow. I spent too many centuries in a world with razors that could slice your hee-haw off. We are not dealing with the jungle. Drapes alone are fine. No carpet required.*

Okay, okay! Katie put up her hands. *Just asking. I mean, I don't mind. Women pay thousands of dollars for treatments to stop hair growth. I got mine for the small price of sharing my body with a demon.*

See? Pandora retorted. *Always look on the bright side of life.*

Katie laughed and finished up, stepping out and drying herself off.

She pulled on some sweatpants and a tank top and brushed her wet hair before throwing it into a messy bun. She wandered out to the kitchen and made her special sugary popcorn, this time in orange, then grabbed a bottle of water and headed to the family room. Eric, Derek, Stephanie, and Calvin were already there, waiting to turn on the new hundred and ten-inch flat screen television Korbin had surprised the group with. Derek had taken the time to hook up some badass speakers and wired them around the room to create almost a movie theatre setting, only with a comfortable couch and big comfy armchairs.

"All right, crew, are we ready?" Derek asked, clicking on the television and looking at everyone.

Calvin pointed to the screen. "Make it so, Number One," he intoned.

They all sat back as the soaps began, humming along to the intro. As they watched they cracked jokes, their laughter a familiar and warm sound in the space.

Katie was starting to think she liked the time with her team more than she liked the soaps themselves. Of course, Pandora would argue that any day of the week. Just as the second scene came on her phone buzzed in her pocket. Katie pulled it out and smiled at Ella's name on the screen.

Dude, are you watching the soap? Ella texted.

Yeah, we are all here watching, Katie replied.

Holy shit, did you see what Eddie did to Veronika?

Stop! Stop right there, Katie texted. **NO SPOILERS! We are just now watching it!**

Okay, okay, Ella texted. **I'm rewinding so I can watch with you**.

She stared at the screen as Eddie, one of the main characters, turned to Veronika and smiled, holding a knife behind his back. Everyone slid to the edges of their seats as they waited to see what would happen. As Eddie brushed his hand across Veronika's sweet pink cheek, he jabbed the knife into her stomach. Tears fell from Veronika's eyes as she looked longingly at Eddie.

"I…just…wanted…to love you," Veronika sputtered.

HOLY SHIT! Katie texted to Ella. **He stabbed the bitch! I KNOW!!** Ella texted back. **Like, holy shit is right.**

That bitch was crazy though, all "oh but I love you, Eddie." Please! I would have kicked his ass.

Slow down, Katie texted back, laughing. **But you're right, he deserves an ass-kicking. And he is fucking crying! Why is he crying?**

Right?! If you wanted to keep her, you shouldn't have stabbed her, Ella replied with an angry-face emoji.

Boys are dumb, Katie wrote back.

That they are, Ella responded.

The story continued, and everyone waited with bated breath as Veronika was carried, almost dead, into the void. The show ended there, but they had several more episodes to go. Derek shook his head and put his hands in the air.

"Ten bucks says she comes back to life as some wild and crazy bitch and slaughters everyone," Derek offered.

"No way." Stephanie snorted. "That bitch is going to be stupid and fix Eddie's problems and come back to him like, 'Oh, I understand that the aliens wanted you to kill me. It's okay, I forgive you.' Bitch, *please*! He stabbed your ass."

"Fucking white people," Calvin replied shaking his head. "The Queen Bitch would have whupped his ass and sent him back to the aliens with his balls around his damn neck. Then she would have taken his Mercedes and lived a nice comfortable life in the hills."

Katie laughed as the next episode started. Stephanie shushed everyone, and Eric plopped down on one side of the couch, then moved in for a closer view. He snatched some orange popcorn from the bowl and smiled at Katie.

"Be careful with that." Stephanie chuckled. "That demon is likely to snatch your hand right off your arm."

Damned right, Pandora grumbled.

A flash of light sparked, sending energy surging across the small Arizona town. Moloch growled as he swung open the cast iron gate to hell and stepped out into the moonlight.

He looked down at the dusty town below, grimacing at the thought of being there any longer than he had to. Humans were ignorant. They loved the dusty hot waste-land of the West, but hated the idea of the dusty wastelands of hell. At least in hell he could torture whoever he wanted. Here he had to keep a low profile until it was time.

Moloch was there to talk to the survivalist group, to continue his plan to help T'Chezz take over Earth. He had gone through its members, picking out six men who would fit the bill for his team. The rest would be servants, making sure things went as planned and sacrificing themselves to the bigger picture if necessary.

The men he chose were all strong, stout humans, already physically capable and open to allowing their demon to take control.

All they were waiting on were the actual demons.

Moloch had taken care to choose demons who would create maximum havoc, provide the highest possibility of success, and didn't take shit from anyone. They had volun-teered—under strenuous pressure from Moloch—and had traveled inside him to Earth.

They would meet their new capsules very soon, and when they did training would commence. Moloch opened the door to the house where the cult lived, watching as everyone stood at attention. The six men nodded and followed Moloch back to the spell room. Lit candles surrounded the space, casting flickering ominous shadows against the walls.

"I have brought you your demons," Moloch growled.

The men lined up and stood straight with their hands clasped in front of them. Moloch approached each, breathing the soul of the chosen demon into the human body. The newly infected's head would tilt back and drop forward as the demon situated itself inside. Once all had received their demon, the six men looked at Moloch. Their eyes glowed bright red as their muscles twitched and strengthened. The demons were already modifying their humans, making them as strong as they could for the moment.

Demons thought of the human body as armor. The longer it took to get through that armor, the longer the demon stayed on Earth.

"You are now holding the keys to all of our futures," Moloch told them. "Your sacrifices will not go unnoticed, and when the task is done you will be rewarded for your valor."

Even as Moloch spoke of rewards, he knew that he would dispose of these humans when he was done with them, keeping their souls for the fireplace in his office.

They were nothing to him, but he knew how the human mind worked. To get them to cooperate, he had to stroke their egos.

He was capable of controlling men better than women, since females were more grounded in their own thoughts. That was why he used the women as watchers, but turned these six strong men into demon beings.

Moloch paced in front of the men. "These so-called Damned have been exterminating our kind for far too long. They have grown stronger and smarter, and have learned to manipulate demons for personal gain. This is not only defiant, but disrespectful to our Master. We will no longer stand by and allow our brothers and sisters to be sacrificed for man's greed. If they refuse to share we will take it all, and we will leave no man standing!"

The six men let out a battle cry and shook their heads, but the others cowered in the back, wondering if they had made a mistake. Moloch seemed stronger and more powerful than before; his stature dwarfed the newly possessed.

Moloch sneered at the humans cowering in the corner.

"Look at them," Moloch demanded, pointing at a girl who had sunken down and was crying. "They are weak! They are letting their fear rule them, but we embrace our fear and allow it to give us even more power. It is time these Damned know what it is to fight those who freely accept the gift of the *Enlightened*."

Moloch clapped his large hands together loudly. "Demons! Come forth."

The human bodies moved and shifted and the demons' apparitions flickered and shimmered in the faces of the six men. They hissed and growled to show reverence to their leader. They were ready—just as ready as the humans they had overtaken—to set forth on and accomplish their missions. They wanted a place in Moloch's favor just as Moloch wanted one with Lucifer, and they were ready to do whatever they could to make that happen.

"Demons," Moloch growled, "enhance your hosts. Make

them as strong as they can handle, but allow the humans to fight for themselves. You are training them and boosting their powers; boosting their strengths, but do not completely take over their bodies. We need them to be like the Killers, walking unnoticed among the humans until trouble arises. But this time, *we* are the trouble. I expect you to be strong; there is no room for leniency here. If you are not, I promise you I will remember your lack of diligence and you too will become pretty fixtures on my walls, bound to hell for an eternity of torture."

The demons all nodded and retreated back into their human bodies. The humans raised their heads once again, their eyes shining brighter than before. Their bodies were tense, and they looked ready for a fight. Moloch smiled and ran his eyes over the group.

His chuckles reverberated off the walls. "Be calm, my Enlightened, I will provide you with an opportunity to demonstrate your prowess soon."

Korbin poked his head into the training center, but no one was in there. He hadn't anticipated a crowd that late in the evening, but he hadn't seen anyone in hours. When he went outside he noticed Katie's car, which was covered in sand, parked in the garage, but everything else was just as it had been the last time he saw it.

"Dammit." He scratched his head in frustration. His team was there somewhere; he just had to find the fools.

Then it hit him: the hundred and ten-inch television

had been delivered and Derek had hooked it up earlier that day. They were all in the family room.

He made his way through the tunnels to the family room and smiled when he stepped inside, seeing everyone gathered on the couches and chairs. As he looked at the screen though, his nose crinkled; he was pretty sure the team was watching a soap opera. He hadn't expected Rambo, but this was more than a surprise.

Slowly he crept forward and perched on the arm of the large L-shaped couch that had been delivered, but nobody really noticed he was there. He tilted his head to watch as a young woman with blood on her dress cried and talked to very badly-portrayed aliens.

"Do you go visit aliens with diamonds on your wrist?" Korbin asked.

"*Shhh!*" the group hissed in unison.

Stephanie scooted down the couch and tapped the seat next to her, then motioned with her head for him to sit when he didn't move. He contemplated making a run for it, but he had made a tactical error by coming farther into the room than he should have.

"Sit," she whispered. "I'll help you with your inner female and let you know what you missed in the story, because—let's face it—you have far too much testosterone."

"Yeahhhh, boy." Eric laughed as he glanced at Korbin. "The boss is getting involved in this one. His man-card is waving in the wind."

Derek shrugged. "I'd buckle if a pretty girl asked me to sit next to her."

Stephanie smiled and mouthed, "Thank you." Korbin

sighed and plopped down in the seat, raising his middle fingers in the air as everyone cheered and whistled.

He figured that if this was what the team did together, he might as well get in on the action—though it seemed Damian had been smart and stayed as far away as possible.

Sitting next to Stephanie wasn't too bad of a deal either. He could feel the attraction between them when their thighs touched.

"So, this is Veronika," Stephanie explained. "The aliens kidnapped her boyfriend's son and told him that to get him back he had to kill Veronika, so he stabbed her. Well, Tubu, one of the good aliens showed up just in time and took her through the wormhole and saved her life. Because she is a shmuck she is trying to get the little boy back so she can go back to Eddie and be a family again."

"He stabbed her?" Korbin asked, confused.

"Bitches be *cray cray*!" Calvin shook his head.

16

Geneeral Brushwood stood in his office bathroom with his jacket and shirt hung on the back of the door.

His white tee was as perfectly pressed as the rest of his uniform, and he had a white towel draped around his neck.

His face was covered in shaving cream and he slowly pulled a razor over his skin, trimming his five o' clock shadow. He had been so busy that shaving had taken a back seat, and as an officer in command he needed to look his best at all times—even if he was in the trenches battling it out with the rest of them.

When he had accepted the position with the organization he knew it would be a challenge, but he hadn't thought it would be so hands-on. So much for staying in and not retiring.

This assignment won't be so bad. I'll rest here and make a difference. He swished his razor in the water and took off another couple of rows of whiskers. *What a cockup.*

Tchaikovsky was playing on the radio and he hummed along, trying to take himself to a calmer, more relaxed place. Shaving was one of those things that helped him relax; "me time," as his late wife used to call it. Just as he was really getting into it, a voice spoke his name from inside the office.

"General Brushwood?" Colonel Jehovivich called when she didn't see him.

The general sighed and put down his razor, poking his head out of the open bathroom door with shaving cream still on his face. "This better be good, Colonel."

"There you are, sir. Your secretary was at lunch and I heard the music, so I assumed you were in here and I didn't need to sound the alarm."

"I'm pretty sure that I am more than secure in here, Colonel." The general ducked back into the bathroom to finish shaving. "What is so important that you have to come all the way down from your office to tell me? I have very little alone-time anymore—which is something I would like to eventually remedy—so this better be of the utmost importance. If it isn't, come back later."

"I do apologize for interrupting your private time," she told him. "We got a call I thought you would like to take."

"Is it the President?" he asked.

"No, sir." She smiled.

"Is it God?"

"No, not God, sir." She chuckled.

"Then I don't see the relevance," he replied, leaning out and staring at her.

"Well, you had told me that if either of the mercs from

the Virginia operation ever called to make sure that you were notified," she told him.

The general took the towel from around his neck and wiped the remaining shaving cream from his neck and earlobes. He rinsed his face with warm water, toweled it dry, and grabbed his shirt from the door. As he pulled it over his shoulders he stepped into the office.

"Well, what did they say?" he asked.

"They...well, *she*...is on line six, sir," the colonel replied. "She insisted that she speak to you and only you. She said it would be a top-secret conversation."

"Really," he grumbled, eyeing the colonel.

He walked over to his desk and looked down at the phone, where line six was flashing. He finished buttoning his shirt and put his tie on before sitting down and getting comfortable. He looked at the colonel and motioned for her to shut the door. She scampered across and closed it, slowly making her way back and sitting down in front of him.

He punched the button and put the phone on speaker. "This is General Brushwood."

"General, I don't know if you remember me, but this is Katie from the Las Vegas mercenary team Korbin's Killers," she began. "My colleague and I helped out with the Virginia operations."

"Yes, Katie, how are you?" he asked in a pleasant enough voice, or at least he thought it was.

"I'm well," she replied. "I don't want to take a ton of your time. I know you are a busy man, but I have a new product that I want to share with you. I think you will *really* find it useful."

"All right," he responded. "Where would you like to meet?"

"Well, it needs to be tested. I'd like you to be there for the testing, but I need an operation with demons. Do you have anything going on?"

"I've always got ops with demons." He chuckled. "Right now Louisiana seems to be the hot spot. We've had several incursions in a very short amount of time; a couple of days. I haven't been out there yet, since I just got back from Texas where there was a high-casualty event."

"I heard about that," Katie replied. "I'm sorry for the losses."

"Thank you. As far as the test, let's make it Louisiana."

"Good," Katie agreed sternly. "I'll meet you in New Orleans."

Before he could say a word, she hung up. He looked at the phone and lifted his eyebrows, punching the button to turn off the speaker. He shook his head and sighed as he looked at the colonel.

"I guess we are headed to New Orleans," he told her. "I really need to have a talk with Korbin on polite phone manners. These mercs are like street urchins."

"They do have demons in them, sir," the colonel pointed out.

"Yes," he agreed, rubbing his chin. "They do. Which means we always have to be on guard."

Katie waited in the chapel's doorway as Damian finished up his evening prayers. The place looked amazing, even with his neon cross. He had festooned the walls with deep red draperies, set up tables with candles all over, and had the old pews redone by some of Stephanie's girls. There was even a section at the front where pillows had been placed on the floor for lounging and relaxing.

It looked like a trendy coffee shop rather than a chapel, but it fit Damian's personality perfectly. He didn't play by the rules. He was his own person and believed that his God loved him for that.

Katie appreciated that about him, because he applied that philosophy to everyone in his life. He loved them no matter how weird, crazy, or sinful they were.

When he was done he blew out the candle he was holding and set it back on the table, slowly getting to his feet with a grunt.

Katie chuckled. "Getting old?"

"You don't know the half of it!" He smiled at her. "I wonder if there is a retirement plan for this type of work?"

"Usually nobody makes it that long," Katie replied with a grimace.

"Truth." Damian sighed. "What can I do for you?"

"I need spiritual backup," she told him. "I'm going to the Big Sleazy...*Easy*...shit! I'm going to New Orleans."

"All right." Damian laughed. "When do we leave?"

"Now." She smiled. "Meet me at the chopper."

"Give me ten minutes." He shook his head as he headed toward his room. "Always a surprise with you."

"You love me." She waved over her shoulder as she went in the other direction.

Katie grabbed her bags and went out to the chopper. She handed Damian a set of headphones when he climbed in behind her, and they took off for the airport to take the jet to New Orleans.

"While we are in the air, I figured I would mention that I have two cases of the specialty 9mm bullets; one for us, and one for the general's team."

"Ugh." Damian groaned. "Are you serious?"

"Yes, and before you ask, Korbin knows," Katie told him.

"Do you really think this is a good idea?" He leaned forward and put his hand on Katie's shoulder. "We are giving them the tools to wipe us out."

"They could *always* wipe us out," Katie replied, turning to him. "A bullet to the brain kills human and demon alike. If we are going to move ahead in this war, we need to get past the old animosities and mistrust. We can't fight demons if we are too busy fighting each other."

"That is both true and wise." Damian sighed and leaned back in his seat. "I guess Korbin and me, we have a hard time swallowing it. We have been at this a lot longer than you, and we have been through the changes with different generals; through the animosity and mistrust. Even this new general, he wants our weapons. We know he is snooping around trying to find things out about us. It will be very hard for us to swallow a truce, much less believe that they will be forth-coming afterward. I just have a hard time trusting them."

"Then trust *me*," Katie suggested. "This is my life, my business, and my family. I won't let anyone, government or not, take what is rightfully mine. They will have to pry it from my cold dead hands."

"That is not beneath them," Damian shot back.

"Right, but do you really think Pandora would let that happen?"

"No." Damian chuckled. "They wouldn't know what the fuck hit them."

Damn straight, Pandora agreed. *And you can believe that none of them would have their dicks attached when we were done.*

Wow, always straight for the dick, Katie mused.

I call it my "Peter Principle."

Why? I thought the Peter Principle was related to people rising to their level of incompetence?

No, my *Peter Principle is, if you want a man to know you are serious, good or bad, go for the family jewels. There is absolutely no way he doesn't know you are serious if you have his peter in your hand. The difference is only in the amount of squeezing you are doing.*

So, never any miscommunication?

It's either pleasure or pain. A binary result. And if I rip it off? That's always bad.

Ooookayyyy... Katie returned her attention to Damian, away from the crazy dick-snatcher lady.

"You have my trust," Damian told her. "And I will support you in your endeavor to unite the craziness and forge forward."

"Thank you." Katie smiled. "You'll see why it's a good idea. You just have to be patient."

Korbin watched as Katie and Damian took off in the chopper. He shook his head and ducked back inside to head toward his office.

He wasn't sure why Katie was so hell-bent on making friends with the general, but he knew she was in for a letdown. General Brushwood might be politer than the past leaders, but he was just as conniving, Korbin had seen it in his eyes when he had come to the old base.

They had been snooping; trying to get the secrets, trying to find something to hold over their heads to force the weapons from their grasp.

They are drowning out there, their military teams, and the mercs are all over it. They are trying to keep their heads above water, and making friends with the people who can do the job is the first order of business. After that, it's all about power.

He walked into his office and sat down at his desk, thinking about the general. He wanted the weapons, but he didn't know quite what to do to get his hands on them.

The weapons *were* the power in this situation, or at least Brushwood thought they were. Little did he know if the men couldn't fight, if they were fragile humans, no weapons were going to make them better at demon-killing. They had teams of non-Damned trying to be superheroes, and it just wasn't going to work. He shook his head and looked at a note sitting on top of the mess, which had his name written on it. He picked it up and unfolded it; it had Katie's signature at the end.

Dear Korbin,

I knew this conversation would never happen face to face, so I figured I would write to you. Every day I watch the people on this team. I watch them laugh and cry. I watch them eat and sleep, and I watch them live...and I watch them die.

I see the power of family, and the power of friendships getting us through every part of life. I also notice the bond you and Stephanie have. It's subtle, but everyone sees it. You guys really care about each other. You can try to hide it all day long, but that won't make it go away.

One thing I've learned in this career or life or whatever you want to call it, is that tomorrow is not promised to us.

Hell, I guess no one really does, but it's a crap shoot if we will wake up tomorrow morning.

You have a chance that not all of us will be given, and that is the chance to love again; to feel that bond between two people. I keep asking myself why the hell you wouldn't take it.

You have to realize something: behind all the smiles, all the laughter, all the jokes, are individuals who are all missing something or someone in their lives.

Whether it is a past relationship or a congregation, we are all lonely in one way or another. Sure, we have each other; we have that family bond, but you know as well as I do that it is not the same as that deep-rooted intimacy you get from being in love with someone.

Stephanie will never push you or force you to open your eyes, but I love you both and I can't keep my mouth shut.

Just ask Pandora.

I envy the two of you, having the opportunity to be in each other's lives. To feel that connection with someone; that bond. I am jealous, because I am missing that in my own life.

Don't let her get away, don't wake up one day and wish you had loved her while you had the chance, because you may not have tomorrow.

Love,

Katie

Korbin sighed and set the letter down on his desk, rubbing his hand over his chin. He knew people had noticed the chemistry between him and Stephanie, but he hadn't thought about it the way Katie had explained it.

He knew—maybe better than most—that tomorrow wasn't promised to anyone, and at first that had been exactly the reason he hadn't pursued anything with Stephanie.

He didn't want to get close to someone he could lose at any moment. However, as time passed he had formed that bond; that connection with her that he had told himself not to. If she died tomorrow he would be just as broken-hearted as if his significant other had passed.

He cared about her, but things were complicated. They were stressful and political, and he didn't know if it would be right for him to pull her into that world.

He had noticed Stephanie long before she had changed back into her true self. Even as Mamacita, she'd had a spark that had pulled Korbin in like a magnet. She was loud and funny, and when she cared about something the passion was so strong you couldn't hold it back. Still, taking the next step was terrifying.

And he wasn't sure if he could do it.

17

The Naval Air Station Joint Reserve Base was located just a handful of miles from the French Quarter in New Orleans. The base, which bustled twenty-four hours a day, housed several different branches of the military including the Army, the Marines, and of course the Navy.

On that day there were some third-class petty officers on deck, washing down the runways. They were gathered around the smoke deck taking a small break, watching the planes run in and out of the hangars. They all stared as the G5 jet touched down on the runway and slowly approached the building.

One of the petty officers whistled. "Would you look at that beauty? I've been here three years and two months, and all I've ever seen coming and going were military planes. This is definitely a first. I wonder who's in that thing."

"Probably some high-ranking captain's wife and their

snot-nosed teenage kids," another guy offered with a chuckle. "They always get the VIP treatment around here; like this base is so fucking prestigious."

"You're just a booter," the first guy replied with a laugh. "When'd you get out of basic? Like six months ago?"

"So?" he shot back. "I have my crow, don't I? Same rank as you, and you have almost four years in the service."

"We can't all be fancy FCs put on light duty for a swollen wrist. I mean, how difficult *is* your job, anyway?"

The other guys laughed for a moment, then went silent. The jet's stairs had been deployed and out walked Damian, dressed in his normal long coat, shirt, tie, and dress pants, hat tilted to the side. He walked down the stairs and waited for Katie, who stepped out dressed in all black, her pants tight, her shirt tight, and her body flowing with every step. She just about stunned every man who saw her. When she got to the bottom she gave a little hop, making all the guys clear their throats.

"Jesus, Mary, and Joseph," one guy exclaimed, his cigarette barely hanging onto his lip.

"Who the hell are Father Scary-as-Fuck and his daughter, Hotter-than-Hell?" another wondered.

"I doubt that's his daughter," the first petty officer argued. "I don't think priests are allowed to get anyone pregnant."

"Like it's never happened." The youngest petty officer stared, then shook his head. "I have to say, I'd love to be stuck in a confessional booth with her."

"I'd say my Hail Marys every night," another guy commented.

"You boys are pathetic," the female petty officer as she

pushed to the front. "All right, let me see who this chick is. Holy *shit*, she's hot...and I like dick."

"Fucking told you," the younger guy said smugly. "Hot as hell."

Pandora chuckled, since she could hear the conversation from the plane. They obviously appreciated the fine work she had put into her human; she was proud to say she had sculpted her perfectly. She purred to herself, barely audible to Katie.

My minor modifications have definitely done the trick. She snickered. *The men are falling all over themselves.*

What? Katie asked. *What are you talking about?*

Oh, nothing. Just your fan club over there in that gazebo.

Where? she asked, looking at the guys and watching them turn quickly away, acting like they weren't staring at her tits and ass. *You did this, didn't you?*

Don't know what you're talking about, Pandora replied, playing innocent.

I heard you. You said "minor modifications," Katie growled. *Two cup sizes almost overnight are not 'minor modifications.' You've made them so big and bouncy I can barely pull my shirt over them. I am going to have to start getting clothes specially made for me. I'm going to fucking look like Dolly Parton if you keep this shit up.*

I don't know who that is, but if this Parton lady has nice tits, then hell why not?

She's like ninety years old and still has the tits of a twenty-something, Katie snapped. *And she is respected in her commu-*

nity for her talent. Still, I don't want to be known as "Tits McGee" for the rest of my life. You have got to stop it with the boobs.

May I remind you that you haven't had to wear a bra in months unless you wanted to? Pandora scoffed. *Even then, you could drape a tissue over them and it would do the same thing. At least I tried to make it so your nipples aren't hard all the time. I know how much you'd love that.*

I would murder you with my colon, Katie snarled. *I'd explode my appendix so you would feel terrible.*

Don't act all high and mighty. I saw you checking yourself out in that little t-shirt dress we bought.

All right, Katie snapped. *I admit it. Your augmentation of my breasts has actually been worth it. No more restricting bras, no more lines across my back, no more wires jabbing into my armpit from the bra coming undone. It has been a refreshing bit of freedom. I had to get used to it, but now that I have I enjoy it. They look good all the time.*

See? I know what I am talking about.

No one believes I'm not wearing a bra, though. Katie chuckled. *That lady last week at the store asked me if I was wearing one of those stick-em-on bra things. She couldn't fathom that my breasts were just like that.*

Then she asked where you got your implants done. Pandora laughed. *She didn't believe they were natural. She like argued with you for twenty minutes, ending with that lecture on being proud of who you are and the choices you made for your body. You should have just lied and given her the name of a doctor. Or better yet, given her my name and your cell so we could have caught her trying to book an appointment.*

If you could do this to other women's bodies from mine we

would be billionaires. Katie snorted. *We could call it "Mystic Boob Jobs."*

"*Magic Tits.*" Pandora laughed. *Thank you for calling Magic Tits. Sorry we can't get to the phone right now, but our boobs are too big.*

Katie had to hold back her snickers as she hurried to catch up with Damian.

Dr. Handsy and the Bewitching Boob Job. Pandora laughed. *I crack myself up.*

"I'm Colonel Adams." The man shook Katie's and Damian's hand before leading them past a building.

Katie jogged to keep up with him. She looked down the path they were walking and watched as a Blackhawk landed, keeping its engines running. She didn't realize they would be taken somewhere so quickly, but she also had no idea where the general was.

"I'm your pilot," he told them loudly as they got closer to the chopper.

"Where are we going?" Katie asked.

"We are going to an operation about twenty miles out of town. It started about an hour ago, and the team has already surrounded the place. The general is waiting there for you."

Katie nodded and climbed into the back of the Blackhawk. After she buckled in she put on the headphones, and they lifted off the pad. When they had reached the correct altitude, they zoomed toward the incursion.

"Just relax," the pilot suggested. "We will be there before you can write your name on a paper...*legibly*, that is."

Katie grabbed her backpack and glanced at Damian, who nodded. They had their weapons on them, and both had their one bag. She wasn't quite ready for an incursion, but at that point she didn't have a choice. The general apparently didn't play games. He was waiting for her there, and he would want to test the weapons right away. This was her life though; unexpected, always dangerous, and now political in nature.

"If you look ahead, you can see the plume of smoke," the co-pilot told them. "That is where we are headed. One of the boiler rooms caught fire at the beginning of the incursion, but they report that the sprinkler system put out the blaze. We don't think it had anything to do with the demons."

Katie nodded and leaned back, holding onto the handle next to her head. As the helicopter reached the target they slowed and dropped onto a grassy area about five hundred feet from the building.

Damian slid the door open and jumped out. Katie folded the piece of paper in her hand and leaned forward to drop it into the pilot's lap.

She smiled and winked at him before jumping out of the chopper and running after Damian.

"Oh, shit!" the co-pilot exclaimed. "She gave you her fucking number. Seriously, man, I have no idea how you do that. You said two words to her."

"I guess I just got it that way." He smirked.

"Are you gonna call her?"

"Hell, no! she's one of those possessed fighter chicks.

But *shit* does she have a nice pair of tits on her. It might be worth letting out the inner demon for that."

"*I* would," the co-pilot replied. "Fuck, I'd let anything she wanted out."

"She's probably a one-and-done, too," the pilot mused. "You know, one of those girls who knows what she wants, takes it by the...*dick* in this case and gets hers, then no drama. Wipe your hands clean and walk off."

"I'm already in love." The co-pilot laughed.

They both looked out the window to where she was talking to one of the soldiers. They pointed toward the building and she nodded before glancing back at the helicopter. She smiled and her eyes flashed red as she blew them both a kiss before scurrying after Damian and the soldier.

"Be still my, motherfucking heart," the co-pilot moaned. "I think I just came in my fucking pants."

"That's why you're still single." The pilot laughed. "You gotta finesse a woman; show her who's boss. A girl like that secretly wants to be dominated. She doesn't want to always be in charge. I would definitely do my best to show her who's boss."

"Open the note, man! See if she said anything," the co-pilot demanded.

The pilot unfolded the note and laughed before looking down, then his face dropped and he tilted his head. The co-pilot looked confused, unsure why he was having that reaction. Finally, the pilot held up the paper—and on it was her name, neatly written five times in perfect cursive.

"Fucking hell!" the pilot spluttered. "How did she do that?"

"Thanks for letting me come down here and work with you for the day, man," Calvin said as he looked around Joshua's area. "And I have to say, you decorated this thing like a fucking pro. It's like the Bruce Wayne man cave."

"You like it?" Joshua asked. "A lot of this stuff is my family's. I never had a place big enough to put it, so I kept it in storage. I have one of those brains that can remember details after seeing them just once, so I laid this out just like my father's den was arranged when I was a kid."

"You grew up playing next to a suit of armor?" Calvin laughed. "I grew up in the ghetto *wishing* I had a suit of armor—though I can't really imagine myself strapping this baby on and heading to school. I would definitely have gotten beat up for that shit."

"They could have tried." Joshua laughed. "But I don't think you would have suffered too much."

"True." Calvin chuckled. "But yeah...like I said, thanks. I really didn't want to end up in the IT room again. Don't get me wrong...Derek is my boy, but those computer servers and wires and boxes were driving me fucking mad."

"At least we have the space now to do things like that," Joshua replied. "I mean, I was really nervous to move. I am not very good with change. But when we got here and started to set the place up, I realized just how much room I was going to have. After we moved my dad's stuff in and I started working—and still having space to move around—I realized how lucky I was to get to come to this place."

"Agreed." Calvin nodded. "The old place was great, but mostly because it felt like home. We needed to get bigger, and this was our chance. It was the right move to make, that's for sure."

"I have people helping me now too; people on the payroll," Joshua told him. "They like working for me, and I like having them there. It's a win-win for everyone. I wish things could have happened for a different reason, but I'm glad nonetheless."

"Are you doing stuff?" Calvin asked. "Are you getting out of the man cave and enjoying your free time? It's important that you enjoy life, not just slave away down here making bullets and putting blades on sticks."

Calvin noticed something that looked like Katie's quarterstaff. He picked it up and twisted the end, jumping slightly as blades shot out of the sides. Joshua smiled kindly and carefully took it from him, pressing a button and retracting the knives. Calvin nodded in appreciation and walked away from the tools, not wanting to screw anything up.

"That is for Katie; it's a specialty piece," Joshua explained. "And yeah, I actually have friends and a life for the first time. Tonight we are going into town to gamble and eat at a cheap buffet until we *explode*."

"Nice," Calvin said. "You and the girls?"

"Yeah," Joshua replied, stacking the finished weapons into the cabinet and pressing the button to lower it into the ground. "We figure it's time to let loose a little."

"Why don't I tag along? You know, as backup," Calvin asked. "Because I'm a standup guy like that."

Joshua smirked and eyed him, having a feeling that the buffet wasn't what he was concerned about. The girls were beautiful, but they were like sisters to Joshua. To Calvin, though, they were available. Joshua looked down at the papers on his drawing table. He thought it was funny how Calvin was; it was the first time he had really spent any time with him.

"All right." Joshua smiled. "I think it would probably be safest if you came along—just as backup, of course."

"Sweet," Calvin exclaimed, clapping his hands together. "Vegas nights, baby."

18

Katie blew a kiss at the helicopter pilot, laughing the whole time at the play by play Pandora was giving her about what they were saying.

She couldn't believe how much of a douchebag the guy was, thinking she would ever give a man like him her number. She could smell the cockiness on him from half a mile away.

She caught up with Damian and the soldier, who were walking toward a small area with a table. The general and the colonel were standing there next to the guy who had led the charge in Virginia.

"General." Katie shook his hand.

"Katie." He nodded. "And this is Colonel Jehovivich."

"Nice to meet you," Jehovivich offered, noticing the red ring in her eyes. "I've heard a lot about you."

"Hopefully all good." Katie laughed nervously.

"So far," the colonel replied with a fake chuckle.

She glanced at the soldier who was standing next to

them. He had lost a couple of stripes since the last time she'd seen him, when he was leading their team to 'the level boss' who had kicked his ass.

He was no longer commanding the troops; he was strictly support. In fact, it didn't even look like he would be in the fight. She held back a smirk, remembering how they had thrown him back into the room half-conscious.

He was lucky to be alive, but from the look on his face, he wasn't too thrilled to be standing in front of her.

"This is a pretty big event," the general began. "Not huge—not like the last—but bigger than most we've seen out here. It's a tire factory and only half the workers were here today, so we were able to get all but one to safety. None of the demons have been touched. They are stuck inside, since we barricaded the doors from the outside."

Katie looked at the soldiers holding a bar against the door. Whatever was on the other side was not happy; it kept throwing its weight against the door. The soldiers dug their feet into the gravel and pushed back. Katie sighed and shook her head before looking at the general.

"Could I have a word," Katie glanced at the others, "in private?"

"Of course. Let's step over here out of the excitement. Colonel," he nodded to Jehovivich, "hold down the fort."

"Yes, sir," she agreed, obviously not happy at being dismissed.

Katie and the general walked over by two of the vehicles parked to the side, a military Humvee with the general's flag on the back and a regular sedan that she assumed belonged to the colonel.

She put her bag on the hood of the Humvee and stared

at the general. She was nervous, and she decided she wasn't too fond of the idea of being in politics anymore.

"I know that for a very long time, much longer than I've been on the teams, the relationship between the Damned and the military has sucked," Katie began. "Part of the reason for that is the fact that the Damned are treated as monsters. By the same token, though, I understand the Damned have treated the military with disdain when a normal human wasn't going to make it."

"That is very true," the general agreed. "It's a two-way street, though I have to admit that the prior leaders of this sector weren't very open to working with you guys. I heard it all when I took the post, but luckily it went in one ear and out the other."

Katie nodded and fidgeted with her bag. "Sorry, I don't have much of a sales pitch for my stuff. I kind of fell into the business, and have been riding it by the seat of my pants."

"That's life in general." Brushwood laughed. "Just when we think we have a good grasp on things, something else comes along and knocks the wind out of us."

"I would have thought a man like you had it together." Katie smiled.

"A man like me is really good at pretending," he replied with a wink. "So, what do you have for me?"

She pulled the strings at the top of her bag and reached inside to pull out a white and clear plastic box with a yellow top. She put it down on the hood of the car and looked around, making sure that no one was close enough to hear. In reality this part should have been done in an office or somewhere like that, but they were where they were—and those boys weren't going to be able to hold that door much longer.

"This case includes one hundred 9mm rounds that are going to make your demons stand up and scream in pain, if not die immediately. I'm not sure which is more likely."

"Really?" the general exclaimed, opening the case and running his fingers over the bullets before looking at her. "And your company made these?"

"Yes, sir," Katie replied. "We have a secret way of making weapons—I'm sure you've heard of it—and the metal inside those is toxic to demons. When the bullet goes into the demon's body—and they only have to penetrate the skin by a quarter of an inch—the bullet balloons, releasing the toxic metals. Now, I don't know a lot about human anatomy, much less demon anatomy, but I know it works. The swords and knives we have been using have been a godsend, and the cross that our priest uses has taken down some of the largest demons we have seen thus far. These bullets are pretty much guaranteed to at least knock demons right on their asses."

"And you haven't tried them yet?"

"No, sir. This is their debut on the demon scene." Katie smiled. "I figured since we had to try them out anyway, why not do it together? Make a peace offering, and kill some nasty-ass demons in the process? It's not every day you get to watch your work in action."

"No, it's not," he agreed, picking one up and holding it in front of his face.

The bullet shimmered, just like the swords and knives. The metal was on the inside, but he could sense it. He put the bullet back and looked at the door where the soldiers could barely hold the brace in place.

"Okay, what is your tactical suggestion?" he asked.

Katie looked at him in shock. She hadn't expected him to ask for her advice on the situation. Most of the military folks she had met were too full of themselves to reach out and learn more about what they did. She wiped the shocked look off her face and shrugged her shoulders.

"It's not really my style to tell someone how to run their op," she demurred.

"I understand that one." He smiled. "I know that we, as military leaders… We tend to get pretty protective of our strategies. For some it's pride, but I know that for most it's the fact that every man on our team is under our protection; they are our responsibility. I guess it's kind of the way Korbin feels about his team every time he sends them in somewhere. Losing someone is hard, but losing someone you were responsible for is ten times worse."

"Understood." Katie nodded.

"Still, I am not familiar with this kind of weapon, and since it came from your hands I'd like to have your input on how you would set up the men."

"I'd position two shooters with these bullets," Katie pointed at two locations, "and two with regular rounds close by, and a third to the side with a sword."

"A sword?" the general asked, holding back a chuckle. "I'm sorry, I don't think the military has provided swords in a century."

"I didn't think about that. That's all right, I have one. We make those too, out of the same material as the bullets…just for future reference."

"Right. I will keep that in mind," he replied with a straight face, realizing that she wasn't joking. "Tell me this, though: why a sword when we have so many guns?"

"Well, the rounds may kill them; we don't know yet," Katie explained. "But they *will* fry their brains long enough to cut off their heads. Cutting off the head is a really good way to stop a demon. There is no question if they are dead at that point, although you will know they aren't in any case if they don't turn to dust or back into their human. Anyway, if you cut off their head with one of our swords, you are doing two things: you are saving ammo, whether regular or special, and you are stunning them again so that while you are slicing through they don't reach out and claw you in the gut. See, these bullets are like gold, or even more important than that. Maybe water in the middle of the desert. This shit is *rare*." She shook her head. "No joke."

"How rare?" the general asked.

"Right now? Very." Katie tapped the yellow and white box. "It's taken us over a year to make these, General."

He looked down at the box and back up at her. "Is this the first batch?"

She nodded and waited for him to speak. He realized at that moment that this whole thing hadn't been a game.

That Katie and Korbin's team were actually entrusting them with their secret weapon; brand new technology that could change the way they hunted demons.

She was giving them the opportunity to be on the same playing field—or at least closer to the playing field—as the mercenary teams were. She had given him a weapon that could be used against her, and she had done it without hesitation.

He took a deep breath and turned to the troops, calling two of the soldiers over to collect some of the rounds. He looked back at Katie, and she nodded and slipped the rest of them back into her bag for safekeeping. She handed the bag to Damian and winked before pulling two short swords from the sheaths on her back. The colonel, wide-eyed, stepped back and shook her head. She acted as if she had stumbled into a bad movie.

She only wished it were that simple. Katie lived in a world she didn't recognize sometimes, and the colonel lived in a completely different one.

She went home every night, cooked dinner, and put her feet up. When work was done, so was she. Katie had forgotten how that felt.

On that day, though, she was gonna bring her world right to the colonel and the general, then stand back and watch the aftermath.

She hoped the colonel could take a fucking joke.

The general, before setting up, decided to take the special bullets back from the soldiers and give them regular bullets. He instructed them to shoot to wound if a demon got out, since he wanted to see the full power of the bullets he would be firing.

He looked at Katie who was crouching to the side, one sword over her shoulder and the tip of the other in the dirt at her feet. She nodded at him as the door began to bow. The men with the brace had stepped aside; they knew there was a demon thirsting to get out.

They stared at the door for some time until the banging stopped. Katie slowly stood up and looked around her, knowing demons were smarter than that, and sure enough, a loud crash suddenly rang out. The demon had jumped through the window, sending glass flying everywhere. He landed on his feet, one hand on the ground, looking at the soldiers surrounding him. He snarled and barked when he caught a glimpse of the general at the other side of the walkway by the Humvee, who was standing there cool as a cucumber.

The demon took off toward the general. The team leader called out, and a spray of bullets hit the demon. His body jerked as the bullets hit him in the arms, the legs, the waist; everywhere but the head. He growled, but kept his eyes locked on the general. Brushwood didn't panic, though. Instead he yawned as he pulled a couple of the special bullets from his pocket and loaded his gun. The demon fell to the ground but continued to crawl, hell-bent on making it to the man in charge. The general pushed himself off the Humvee and stepped forward, then raised his gun and aimed. He shook his head before pulling the trigger.

A single bullet flew from the barrel and entered the demon's head, and he wailed and writhed on the ground for only a moment before bursting into dust. The general looked down at his pistol with a gleam in his eye, then raised his head and pointed at three men plus Katie, and Damian. Katie took the bag from the priest and handed the general the box. He pulled out several more bullets and loaded his clip, snapping it back into his gun. He smiled and stamped the dust off his shoes as he looked at Katie. Jehovivich scooted closer to hear what was going on.

"Colonel," the general called, waving her over.

She tried to act like she hadn't been eavesdropping and ran over to him. He nodded at her and back at the group. She already had a bad feeling about all of this.

"The colonel here has intel on the ops, and she knows how I would want this to run," the general told everyone. "As for me, I'm going tactical. What do you guys say we treat this little incursion like a field test? I'm itching to try these bullets out in some real action."

Katie laughed. "Just don't point that at me."

"Scouts' honor," the general promised, holding up two fingers.

Katie knew she shouldn't trust him, and from the look on Damian's face *he* didn't, but she had to stay the course.

If she wanted relations with the military—and she wanted to keep them out of her business—she had to show she trusted them, and that they could trust her. She nodded at the general and followed him toward the building. The colonel sighed and rolled her eyes.

"Great, now he's going all John Wayne on me," she grumbled, looking at the teams spread out around the building. "I'm too old for this shit."

19

Korbin woke up the next morning with Katie's letter and Stephanie on his mind.

She always seemed to be right there simmering in his thoughts, but now it was worse. He knew Katie was right. They never knew where life would take them, and tomorrow might not come.

He was out of practice, though, not having taken anyone on a date since becoming Damned. He had always pushed feelings aside, but with Stephanie he found it utterly impossible to do so.

She was boisterous, loud, and funny, and he had been physically attracted to her from the first moment she had worn that suit and started to feel more like herself again. This Stephanie was definitely more his style: badass attitude and fighting style, and personality to boot.

He got out of bed and took a shower, figuring it was now or never. He needed to talk to her; he'd figure out how to spit the words out.

He got dressed and spritzed on some cologne before heading over to Joshua's building. Korbin figured that was where she would be, since she usually went there first. He passed Derek, who stopped in his tracks and looked at him.

"Are you wearing cologne?" he asked with a raised eyebrow.

"Uh, no." Korbin cleared his throat. "New body wash. Crazy scent."

"Oh." Derek smirked and walked away. "Tell Stephanie I said hello."

Korbin whipped around, shocked that he knew, but he had disappeared around the corner with an armful of books.

Korbin let out a deep breath and clenched his fists, trying not to lose his nerve. He took the elevator up to ground level and stepped out, shielding his eyes from the blowing sand. Quickly he made his way over to Joshua's building and went inside, stomping the sand off his feet in the foyer.

When he was finished he stopped stomping and heard a couple of voices coming from just inside the main room. Carefully he crept to the doorway and stood quietly, recognizing the voices as Stephanie's and Edith's, who was formerly one of her girls. He didn't want to eavesdrop, but he couldn't help it. Stephanie's voice was melodic, almost drawing him into the conversation.

"There are a lot of options for you," Stephanie told the girl. "You finished high school with a decent GPA, so there is always college. You can also stay here and work, or there is the option of going back to your old profession. It's up to you, Edith, but the sky is the limit. It is, after all, your life, and you should do whatever makes you happy."

Korbin leaned against the wall and rubbed his chin as he listened to Stephanie talk. She was kind and gentle, and not once did he hear any judgment in her voice. He could almost picture her tending to her children in another life, answering the world's biggest questions.

It warmed his heart and relieved some of the nerves dancing in his stomach. He hadn't heard her talk to anyone like that before, at least not since she was Mamacita, and that was what he needed to make him realize he was doing the right thing.

"Doing what we were doing...it was really good money," the girl mused. "It was a way off the streets, and it put food on the table and gave me nice things. That's *really* hard to turn away from."

"I understand," Stephanie told her calmly. "At some point beauty fades, though, so you have to have a backup. What is yours?"

"This place," she replied. "Eventually college, maybe. I don't really have it all lined up yet in my head. I know I have a good thing here, but it's dangerous at the same time."

"Your thoughts are on track; they are really smart," Stephanie agreed with a sigh. "Working here will give you skills, and skills are really important out there in the world. College will give you skills too, depending on what you want to get a degree in. Having lived on the streets and worked my way up the business, I know firsthand that prostitution is fast money; it's in your hand that day. I know that helps when you are hungry. But there is more to you than that, and I feel that if you really think about it, you will find that you've outgrown it. As far as safety... Well, hooking isn't any safer than being here. You were in a safer place with me in that house, but it is rough on the streets; in here, not so much. Hell, at least here we have weapons and a willingness to kill."

"But what if something happens again like it did at the old base?"

"I can't sit here and tell you that's not a possibility, but here you can get to safety," Stephanie said. "You go directly to the safety zone—which is even further underground—and they will have to kill all of us before they get to you. If you lock the doors, they won't be able to get inside. There is food and water to last for months, and there are also ways to communicate with the outside world from in there. Tomorrow, when you're free, I'll show you the place."

"Okay," the girl agreed. "And thank you for listening to me. I'm good with what you're saying. I don't want to go back to the old life if I don't have to."

"You never *have* to do anything," Stephanie told her quietly. "There are *always* other options."

"I'm gonna grab breakfast for Joshua. Tell him I'll be back soon if you see him, okay?"

"Absolutely," Stephanie replied.

Korbin moved away from the door and acted as if he was just waiting, smiling at the girl as she walked toward the outside door. He smoothed his shirt and pushed his hair back before going into the room. Stephanie looked up and smiled sweetly, putting down the papers in her hands.

"Hey there!"

"Hi." Korbin smiled. "I couldn't help but overhear that conversation. I have to say, you are *really* good at talking to people. You talked to her like I would imagine a mother would talk to someone."

"I thought I heard someone come in." She winked. "I talk to the girls like they are human beings, that's all. I guess these girls *are* like my children in a way, though. I picked them up at their lowest point, and together with the people we've met along the way, I grew them into strong women capable of a better life."

"Well, you deserve accolades for that." Korbin smiled as she blushed and looked down at the table. He put his hands in his pocket and stared at his shoes for a moment.

"Did you come to see Joshua?" Stephanie asked. "He is out for a bit, but should be back soon."

"No, actually I came to see you," Korbin told her. "I knew you would be over here this morning. I...uh...I wanted to ask you something. I wanted, or I hoped... I..."

Korbin stumbled over his words and Stephanie looked at him with patience. He cleared his throat and let out a deep breath.

"I *suck* at this." He laughed when he looked at her comforting smile. "I wanted to know if you would do me the honor of allowing me to take you on a date?"

"Who are we killing?" she asked with a smile, moving across the room nonchalantly. "I'll have to change. I don't do well in heels on these 'dates.' I *am* surprised that you're taking the helm on an incursion. You usually leave the dirty stuff to us—not that I mind having you out there with me."

"No." Korbin shook his head. "There's no incursion."

"Oh?" Stephanie stared at him. "A single demon? Someone I missed?"

Korbin was starting to get frustrated. He wasn't sure if she was doing it to be a jerk or if she actually had no clue he was hitting on her. He shook his head and bit the corner of his mouth, trying to figure out how to explain what he was talking about.

He was so slow at these things; part of him couldn't blame her for not believing he was hitting on her. He had given her no signs that he was interested in the first place.

"There's no killing to be done," Korbin continued, catching her stare.

"No killi— Oh!" You could see the lightbulb go off in Stephanie's head when she realized he was talking about an actual date, not an incursion "date." She threw her head back and laughed, but quieted down when she saw his reaction.

"I'm not laughing at you." She smiled. "I'm laughing at myself for being so dense. I thought you meant an incursion, like when Katie talks about her and Damian's first 'date' at the exorcism. I'm sorry, Korbin. I just made a fool of myself. I would be honored for you to take me on a date. Hell, I've been *waiting long enough for you to ask*."

"Apparently you didn't think I would." He chuckled. "And it took a lot for me to come down here, so you might have been right."

"What made you change your mind?" she asked, leaning against the chair.

"A sign from God." He thought about the note. "I just didn't want life to whizz past us without giving it a shot. We work well together, and I want to see where it can go."

"That's the most unromantic thing anyone has ever said to me," she told him, looking down. "But I like it. No bull-shit, no games; just honesty."

"I'm not much for bullshit," he admitted.

"All right, Korbin, when would you like to take me out?" she asked.

"I was thinking like three days from now," he suggested, looking at his watch. "It's Thursday, so let's say Sunday evening. Everyone else will be here relaxing, and we can sneak out for some good food and good conversation."

"That is the pathway to my heart." She laughed. "And Sunday sounds perfect. We can end our weekend with a bang, and not the kind that comes from the barrel of a gun either."

"Exactly." Korbin smiled.

Bullets whizzed through the hallways, hitting demons left and right. Katie ran through the dusty explosions to grab others and break their necks faster than the soldiers could follow. Katie was sure glad they had come along. There were so many of them; the military wouldn't have lasted ten minutes. She was working up a sweat, even with Pandora's juicing. She ran forward and leaped off a pile of debris, feet forward, toward another demon. She locked her legs around him and grabbed his head, pausing only for a moment before snapping his neck. The demon turned to dust and she landed on the ground, one knee down and a hand in the pile of ash.

"Yuck." She grimaced and stood up to wipe the ash off her pants.

"Better than a handful of guts," Damian countered as he came up beside her.

"True," Katie agreed. "Come on, there are about six of these bastards in the lab over here."

Damian nodded and took off behind Katie, his gun out and ready to fire. He was slower than she was, and by the time he got into the lab—fifteen seconds after her— she was slicing the last demon's throat. He shook his head and smirked, never having seen her move that fast before. He opened his mouth to congratulate her but found himself plummeting to the floor with a demon snarling in his ear.

He grunted and rolled when his shoulder met the hard floor, turning onto his back to look up at the beast. Its eyes gleamed red and its claws were curved to strike. Damian chuckled at the surprise on the demon's face as he raised his gun. He curved his mouth into a huge grin and pulled the trigger, blowing the demon's head clear off. Blood sprayed, but before it could reach Damian's face it turned to dust.

"Now I'm *really* glad it's not guts," Damian told Katie, blowing the dust from his lips.

Katie laughed and pulled Damian to his feet. Before he was all the way up the door burst open and Katie raised her gun, crossing it over her outstretched arm. The soldier coming through immediately put his hands up, seeing the barrel of her gun pointed at his head. She let out a deep breath and put her weapon back in its holster.

"How's it going out there?" Katie asked.

"We killed a few," the soldier told her, looking around at the seven piles of ash. "I see you killed a few too."

"Eh." Katie shrugged and swiped the ash from her shoulders. "A few."

"Well, there are two big ones headed our way," the soldier advised them. "We need you."

"It's nice to be needed," Katie replied, glancing at Damian.

Damian nodded and walked toward the door, pulling his cross from the inside pocket of his coat.

"A couple more won't kill us." Damian grinned.

Katie raised an eyebrow and followed them.

"I hope," he amended.

20

T he general pressed his back against the wall, raising his gun and shoving another clip of the special bullets into it.

He took a deep breath and slowly peeked around the corner.

Two large demons had caught wind of them and were stalking them through the halls. They had split up, Katie and Damian leading one in one direction while the soldiers and the general got the other one to follow their trail. The beast was huge and strong, and had already taken down one of his men with a single blow from his fist.

He motioned to the soldiers that the coast was clear and they moved down the next hallway, checking the rooms along the way.

When they had cleared the last of the rooms they stopped and motioned to the general, who was slowly creeping down the hall with his gun at the ready.

Just when he was about to reach them the demon turned the corner, its head barely missing the ceiling.

The soldiers opened fire as they backed away from the beast. The general waited for the beast to slow, watching as black blood began to seep from a few of the wounds. He aimed at the beast's chest and pulled the trigger, watching as the special bullet bored into him.

The beast wailed as it raised its arms and threw its head back. It was stunned, and stumbled backward before crashing to the ground. The general didn't hesitate; he marched forward and aimed at the demon's head.

As soon as the beast lifted his chin, the general blasted him. The demon's eyes flashed red, and his body shook until it was still; not dead, but no longer moving.

There was a loud crash behind him and he whirled, raising an eyebrow. The soldiers, who were breathing heavily, leaned against the walls and looked at the general, who nodded at them.

Katie and Damian had been superstars when they had first entered the building, taking down demons faster than the soldiers could raise their guns. Now *they* were struggling? He didn't believe it. This demon was big, but they had already taken theirs down. He took a step forward, but stopped on hearing another loud crash.

He decided it was probably better to leave them to it than to run in with guns blazing. The last thing he wanted to do at that moment was accidentally take one of them out. That would definitely not help the military-mercenary relationship.

He looked at the soldiers and shrugged, then pulled a box away from the wall and sat down. He would just wait this one out. After about ten minutes a loud wail filled the hallway, then silence.

The general stood and the soldiers gathered behind him as they waited for the approaching footsteps. The doors to the hallway swung open and in walked Katie and Damian, covered in ash, sweat beading their foreheads. The general laughed, clapping his hands together.

"Good job. We got em all."

"Not all of them," Katie said, pointing behind the general.

The military contingent swung around and stared as the demon glared at them with red eyes. Apparently, he hadn't been down for the count. He had only stayed out until the effects of the metal in the bullets wore off. The beast roared, and the gust blew the general's hat off his head. He lifted his gun and shot three times, each shot striking the beast's skull. He groaned and growled, then his red eyes rolled back in his head and his body collapsed. The beast died before he could hit the floor, and a pile of ash plumed into the air.

"Okay," the general told them as he turned back around, "*now* we got 'em all. Lesson learned: never leave a live demon behind you."

The general, the soldiers, and Katie and Damian went back through the entire building, double-checking every room. When they had cleared the last space, the general nodded and put his gun back into his holster. He walked the two Killers back outside and smiled at the soldiers, who were giving them a round of applause.

"These bullets are fucking fantastic," he whispered to Katie.

He pulled the two of them over to the Humvee where they had originally talked. The soldiers went to work cleaning up some of the mess while the colonel walked over to them shaking her head. Katie could tell she wasn't pleased with how the general had run off, but there was nothing she could do about it.

"Okay, this is where I hear the bad news," the general said quietly. "How expensive and how crappy are the terms you are looking for?"

Katie glanced at Damian, then across the field. The general still didn't get it; he still didn't understand why she was there. She sighed and leaned in, not wanting to speak too loudly.

"We aren't looking to make a lot of profit," Katie said. "I need you to understand something: for the sake of war, we all need to make friends out of enemies."

"I agree," the general replied.

"I don't know if you really understand," Katie said. "I am not going to give up my company, and if the government tries to take it the results won't be pretty. In reality, they can't just take it because there is really nothing to take. There is one man; it's a one-man show, and you can't force that man—who is working for me and loyal to me—to do anything he doesn't want to do. Unless of course you are good with slavery?"

Katie lifted an eyebrow and stared at the general, who was looking coldly at her with a straight face. The conversation had shifted; it was no longer about friendships, it was about preserving the company everyone had worked so hard on.

It was about preserving the tools they needed to get ahead of the game and kill these demons, and to face the army that would soon be approaching their doorsteps.

The general didn't know any of this, though. All he knew was what he saw, and that was an increase in demon activity from one shore to the other. He saw a military incapable of handling a mass invasion, even with special bullets and magical swords.

He saw certain defeat without the right alliances, and although Katie wasn't looking for military allies, she was also not looking for a fight.

"I'm not sure I know what you mean," the general told her.

"Not that we are even considering this," the colonel spoke up, "but capturing a demon-infested person is not technically holding them captive. We would be protecting them and the people they could possibly injure. We are willing to do that with any of the infected, no matter what their rank or stature."

"Are you *threatening* me, Colonel?" Katie asked, her eyes flashing. "Because I don't really think that is a smart move."

"All right, you two!" The general stepped forward. "No need to bicker. However, if you want to look at it as a technicality, the colonel is right. It would not be considered holding a human against their will if they weren't completely human."

"Except my guy is not Damned." Katie smirked at the colonel. "He is an innocent. He is clean, and he has been his whole life. And if you decide to take him against his will? Well, I'll come get him."

Damian blew out a deep breath, and Katie could tell he was holding back a look of panic. The general squinted at Katie and stepped forward again to stand toe to toe with her. Katie was nervous, but she didn't flinch. She knew that would be the worst thing she could do.

"Now, now, Miss Maddison," he said. "Who is threatening whom now?"

"It's not a threat, General Brushwood." She smiled, not giving a damn that he knew her last name or that he had just proven he was checking up on the mercs. "I'm just telling you that I would do the right thing in that situation. You don't leave your men behind, whether they are fighters or not. I think you underestimate the family bond the mercenaries have. Not one of our team, or any of the other teams, would feel okay leaving him in your hands against his will. That has nothing to do with the weapons; that's just because he is *family*. Throw in the weapons, and you would have a really big fight on your hands."

Pandora growled. *Fucking tell him he better not go anywhere near that kid.*

"Think about it," Katie continued, standing back up straight. "Allowing him to remain a hostage to a terrorist organization wouldn't be the right thing to do at all."

"Now hold on just a minute!" the colonel exclaimed. "'Terrorist organization?'"

Katie turned her head. "That's what you call organizations or militaries in other countries who kidnap people and hold them against their will for political gain, right?" Katie asked. "If you would label someone else that way,

why would I not label this branch of the military as terror-
ists if they unlawfully took someone hostage in order to
gain both military and political benefits?"

"Anything this military does or doesn't do is strictly for
the betterment of the country," Jehovivich snarled.

"Right." Katie chuckled. "I may not be that old, but I can
tell you that politics is politics, and sometimes it has more
to do with what you line your pockets with and less to do
with national safety."

"All right," the general snapped sternly. "You really
know how to hit below the belt, kid."

"General," the colonel gasped.

"Come on, Colonel, you can't be that blind to how
things work in the highest ranks? You've been in a long
time," the general told her. "You more than anyone should
understand that not everything is a hundred percent for
the safety and the well-being of this country, even though I
wish I could say it was. Why do you think that this position
comes open so much? The previous leaders got greedy.
They got power hungry, and they made choices based on
what would bring them the most money, power, or pres-
tige. It's not rocket science."

"Still, *we aren't a terrorist organization,*" the colonel
replied, stepping back angrily.

"Might doesn't make right," Katie replied. "Right is the
only thing that makes right. Might tried to force the right
results sometimes, and when that happens good men and
women—and I include myself as a good woman—fix it. We
don't step aside and let the tide roll how we want it to. We
stride forward, and we don't allow anyone to stand in our
way. For us this is about family and you are the outside

person in that equation. It's not the demons speaking for us, or the politics; it's just us—the Killers, the ones who see the action, who understand the rage, who fight our instincts to protect people like the two of you."

Damian nodded at Katie and looked at the general, who was obviously thinking about what she had said.

Katie was right; you had to stay the course in their line of work. You had to do things because they were right, not because they offered the biggest payout.

That was where these guys had gone wrong; they had seen that firsthand in Virginia. That lead officer would never make that mistake again, even if he were ever back in that position.

"All right." The general sighed. "Let's reach an agreement, I don't want this animosity to continue longer than it already has."

Katie smiled and walked closer the general as he pulled a sheet of paper from his pocket and took the pen the colonel reluctantly handed to him. Katie could tell she was completely against this alliance, but her opinion didn't matter. The general knew that Katie had the key to his sector's success, and if they tried to take that key they would find themselves backed into a corner by a pack of rabid mercenaries.

That was the last thing that he wanted, and the last thing that Katie wanted to see happen. This would give them the opportunity to share resources and help each other, because she knew that one day they might need each other's help. The demons were rising, and she wasn't going to just sit around and wait for them to show up.

eneral Brushwood thrust his hand toward Katie as the colonel folded the paper and put it into her inner coat pocket. Katie looked down at his hand and back up at his face, unsure for a moment that she wasn't making a deal with the devil himself.

She had come there for that purpose—to make a deal to get the general off their asses and to secure her company's future under her name—and this was what she had been waiting on. She sighed and finally reached out, firmly grasped his hand, and shook.

Pandora gave her a little juice and the general pulled back, rubbing his hand and chuckling.

Katie smiled and nodded at Damian. He unzipped his bag and pulled out another yellow-topped container, looking at the general for a moment before handing it to Katie. She set it on the hood of the Humvee and looked at the colonel before turning back to the general.

"That is the second box of rounds we've made," she told

the general as he picked the box up and popped the lid open. "That's two-thirds of our stock, so don't waste them. I don't know how long it will take for the company to make more. With just one man working on it, it could take months. When more become available we will let you know."

"What about *your* team?" the general asked.

Katie smirked. "I am pretty sure that we will get along just fine with one box for now. We have skill sets that exceed magic bullets. Your soldiers do not, which means that right now you need them more than we do. If the situation changes or the tables turn we will let you know, but for now take them, use them wisely, and for fuck's sake get some Damned on your teams. These boys aren't going to make it otherwise."

"I would if I could," the general said regretfully. "It's not allowed in our service."

"Your loss." Katie shrugged and turned to walk away.

"Wait," the general said. "You still haven't told me what you want. You outlined the entire deal with me, minus what your expectations are."

"That will come," Katie told him, pursing her lips. "But for now, don't die. I really don't want to restart negotiations with some new fucktard. And don't try to tell me otherwise; I've heard the stories about the last few men in your shoes."

The general nodded at the colonel and she hurried after Katie and Damian. She jogged behind them through the grass in her heels, finally catching up when they were almost to the helicopter. Katie could tell she wanted to ask a question, and although she now despised the woman, she knew she had to play nice until she got herself off those grounds.

She looked at the colonel and lifted her eyebrows.

"I have been wondering since I left your base: just how large was that demon you fought back in Vegas? You know, the one who took out the sides of all of those abandoned buildings?"

"I know what you're talking about," Katie told her, staring straight ahead.

Katie knew it had been too good to be true; that the visit to the old base had ended without any more questions.

This colonel though; she was a smart one. She had figured out more than what she had been told about the fight at the base. She had read between the lines, and that in itself was impressive.

Katie had to answer, especially since the general had a loaded gun in his holster filled with bullets that would demolish her and Pandora. She couldn't tell her the truth; he would immediately take her down.

It wasn't their business anyway. The Killers were a private organization just like the other mercenary teams, and they didn't have to answer to the military. She was fishing, but Katie had to give her something—even if it was incredibly far from what had actually happened. This colonel hadn't given up yet, and she wasn't going to stop just because Katie didn't want to answer her.

"Pretty damned big," Katie replied shortly.

"How did you kill it, then?" the colonel asked as they reached the helicopter.

Katie stopped and glanced at Damian, who stopped

abruptly as well. A smirk moved across her lips as she stared at the colonel, who was hell-bent on being a little too inquisitive. Katie wasn't going to lie to the woman; she just wasn't going to give her the whole story.

"Actually, *I* didn't kill it," Katie told the woman. "His cross did. He pressed it against the demon's head and it melted straight through his skull. The demon just turned to dust after that."

Damian pulled out the cross and held it up for the colonel to see. He smiled at it, remembering exactly what happened that day. She tilted her head and reached toward it, but Damian winked and put it back into his pocket.

"Fucker choked to death on it." Damian grinned. "Fitting, right?"

Katie laughed and the colonel stepped back, putting her hand up to block the dirt blowing around under the helicopter's blades.

Katie and Damian climbed into the chopper and the colonel watched as it lifted into the air and flew away. Jehovivich stayed where she was until they were completely out of sight, thinking about what Katie had told her. She chuckled and walked toward the Humvee.

"I didn't know priests swore," she mumbled.

As she started back across the lawn the general, holding his two cases of bullets protectively, piled into the Humvee. She snorted lightly, wondering where the wild cowboy had gone. Suddenly she stopped in her tracks and turned back toward the makeshift helo pad with her mouth wide open.

"Interesting," she whispered to herself.

The colonel had just realized that Katie had bypassed the actual question and given her half an answer.

The Killer hadn't told her how big the demon had been. She'd deflected, passing the buck to the priest—whom she knew wouldn't ever be interrogated by the government.

He was a man of the cloth and therefore had immunity, but Katie—she was playing with fire, and the colonel was determined to watch her burn.

———

When Katie and Damian got back to base that night everyone was waiting for them. They weren't there because they were so interested in what was going on or to ask where the hell they had been; they were all waiting to hit the bar.

Katie was tired, but she couldn't deny that the looks on their faces were priceless.

Derek stood with his palms together and his bottom lip sticking out. Eric was biting his lip and standing as if he were a child waiting for a big surprise. Calvin stood in the background, fixing the collar of his shirt and trying to look extra nice, and Stephanie and Korbin were talking quietly to each other behind everyone.

Finally Katie gave in, and she laughed when the group cheered. They loaded up in the SUVs and headed to Torn Asunder, which was their favorite bar.

Amy's Assassins were there that night, partying it up like always. Everyone but Katie and Damian were on the dance floor; Katie was watching the fights breaking out all over the place. It was the same as always; never a dull moment, and never a steady piece of furniture either.

As she scanned the room, her eyes latched with a pair of

blue ones across the way. She looked away, then looked at the rest of him. She recognized him from the time they had gone to look at weapons, but she had no idea who he was besides a member of Amy's Assassins.

He was handsome though, standing over six feet tall with broad shoulders, big muscles, and an ass that was tight as hell. His chin was perfectly chiseled, and his dirty-blond hair was meticulously styled.

He was standing with a group by Amy, but he couldn't seem to keep his eyes off Katie. She blushed and turned to talk to Damian, but his headphones were in so she grumbled and turned back—to find herself staring directly into someone's crotch. She turned her head and stood up, confused and thrown off her guard.

"I'm sorry," a deep and manly voice said. "I didn't mean to scare you."

Katie shook her head and ran her eyes up the guy's body to his face, realizing it was the one from across the room. She cleared her throat and smiled.

"It's all right." Katie shook her head. "I just didn't see you there."

"I saw *you*." He smiled. "In fact, I was hoping you would like to dance."

"Dance?" she repeated, lost in his baby-blue eyes.

"Yeah. You know, like the others?" He chuckled, nodding to the people on the dance floor.

She giggled. "Sure, let's dance."

Oh god, Pandora groaned. *I don't even know if you can dance. Of all the nights you decide to get frisky, you have to do it when I'm barely focused.*

Just make me look good, Katie hissed.

That I've already done. You are bouncy and perfect, as always. Pandora yawned.

Katie smiled as they reached the dance floor and he put his hand on her waist. The music wasn't necessarily slow, but she was going to pretend that it was, just for argument's sake. She liked being that close to a man, and especially since he happened to be handsome and new to her. He had caught her off-guard which was something that never happened to her. She was always in control of things, but at that moment on the dance floor she just kind of let go. She could feel everyone staring, giggling, talking about her dancing with a stranger, but her eyes were too busy devouring his to care about any of that.

"I'm Noah," he told her in the smoothest voice she'd ever heard. "Noah Rappley. I'm on Amy's team."

"Nice to meet you, Noah," she replied, trying to get hold of herself. "I'm Katie, of Korbin's Killers."

"I know." he chuckled. "You are somewhat of a legend around here."

"Lord, I'm not old enough to be a legend." She grimaced.

He backtracked. "Well, maybe not a legend, but everyone knows who you are."

"Right." Katie smiled. "I'm glad you had the guts to come talk to me, then."

"It took a while to gather my nerve." he chuckled.

Katie smiled and stared at his chest. Her hand was in his, and they danced to the beat of their own drums. She liked what was going on, but the bar wasn't her scene and she wanted to get to know Noah better.

"You wouldn't happen to like four-wheeling, would you?"

"Are you kidding?" He laughed. "I love it! I used to do it with my brothers all the time before...you know." He gestured to the bar. "All of this."

"How about we get out of here and go do some?" She had a glint of mischief in her eye.

"That sounds *perfect*," he agreed.

She smiled and pulled him off the dance floor. Pandora had given her a bit of juice, pushing her to get the hell out of that bar so he was more than surprised to almost fall over as her little body—well, compared to his—yanked him away from the crowd. She grabbed her bag and looked at Damian, who looked up from his book with a lifted eyebrow. Katie smiled broadly and kissed him on the cheek, not saying a word as they rushed from the bar. She was very glad she had decided to take her truck that night. Noah's mouth hung open as she beeped the alarm and got into the driver's seat.

"Nice," he said, climbing into the passenger side and buckling his seatbelt.

"I know the perfect place to have some fun," she told him excitedly.

She headed out to the desert about forty-five minutes outside of town. When she found the turnoff she and Derek had taken, she pulled off the road and up into the hills, laughing as he held on tightly with a wild look in his eye.

They had an amazing time, taking turns running through the sand, jumping over the hills, and coming to a sliding halt on the other side. She liked how he looked in her truck, his big muscles tensing and relaxing as she alternately hit the brakes and slammed the gas down.

Finally she left the sand and headed for the mountainous terrain, driving up the slope as she'd done before. They sat there on the lookout talking about what they had just done, both their bellies hurting from laughing so much. When they were finally quiet, Katie couldn't help but notice that he hadn't made a move yet and she worried that he had lost interest. She didn't need another brother; she had plenty of them.

He's interested, Pandora hissed.

How do you know? Katie asked. *He hasn't tried anything.*

He has a sign. It's in his pants, and it's ten inches long and about six fucking inches in diameter, Pandora told her. *Unless it's a sock. Holy shit, if that's a sock I'm going to be pissed.*

I doubt he wore a huge stuffed sock in his pants to the bar, Katie replied, exasperated.

You never know with men. It's like socks in the bra, padding to look more desirable. Either way, it's got the words "jump me" written all over it.

You don't know that, Katie responded, sitting awkwardly next to him.

He smiled and took her hand. His hands were surprisingly smooth and gentle, and she could feel the electricity pulsing through her body. She hadn't had that feeling in a very long time, and had almost forgotten what it was like to be nearly breathless from just holding a man's hand.

Seriously? Pandora asked, sniffing their hormones. *I don't know what else you want. You are too damned confused for this century. You want to be treated like an equal, you want to do one thing on Monday, but something different if it's a full moon.*

Tuesday is completely off the charts, and you want him to read your fucking inscrutable mind. I swear, I now understand exactly why the book was written.

What book? Katie snapped.

Men Are from Mars, Women Are from Venus. Pandora sighed. *More like women are from hell. I'm so glad I'm not a man in this century.*

He is acting totally appropriately, and not pushing anything on me whatsofuckingever, Katie argued. *Which, I might add, is exactly how a man is supposed to behave toward a woman. Why are you snapping at me?*

Because you are whining in my ear about wanting to know his intentions and annoying the hell out of me, Pandora said. *It is very obvious what he wants. He's a guy! What do you THINK he wants?*

Not all guys are the same, Katie argued. *Maybe he's a gentleman.*

Oh, please. Pandora scoffed. *That snake in his pants is a big indicator. Ask him if he wants to fuck, because tomorrow you both might die.*

I can't handle you right now, Katie growled.

"Katie?" he said, making her jump.

"Mmmhmm?" she replied, trying to push the image of his manhood out of her mind.

"Do you like this life?" he asked. "Are you fulfilled?"

"I, uh, am I filled? I mean, *ful*filled? In some ways I am very much fulfilled," she answered, trying not to blush. "Are you?"

"In ways, yeah," he agreed. "But sometimes I miss the idea of a partner. You know, a woman to spend my time with. Someone who can be my best friend."

Oh boy, Pandora groaned. *He is laying it on thick. Hey buddy! You don't need to say all that stuff. Just touch her hoo-ha, and it's in the bag!*

Shush, Katie chastised her.

"I don't know." He laughed and looked out the window. "Maybe it's just the old times rearing their ugly head again. It's probably stupid."

"It's not stupid." Katie smiled and gripped his hand tighter. "We are still human. We still crave that closeness; that relationship. We still want the same things we wanted before, we just have to figure them out in a different way."

"You're right." He smiled. "You're definitely right. I like sitting out here with you. I feel normal—like a regular guy hanging out with a beautiful woman."

Oh yeah, I feel you buckling under the pressure already. Pandora laughed.

Be quiet, Katie demanded. *I am not going to sleep with him.*

In the darkness of the mountain, all you could hear was the sound of a zipper slowly being pulled down. Insects chirped from the bushes as Katie lay in the back of her Raptor, wrapped in the arms of a big burly man. Pandora was in seventh heaven.

ABOUT DAMNED TIME, she yelled.

Oh gawd, Pandora gasped. *That's bigger than... Well, that's a big-ass snake.*

Shut the fuck up, Katie mentally shrieked.

22

Stephanie stood at the kitchen counter staring at the pot of coffee, trying to keep her eyes open long enough to find a cup.

She had definitely drunk way too much the night before, and though her hangovers were usually pretty mild, that morning she felt like she had been at a rager all night. She forgot that when you dance the night away you tend to forget how much alcohol you have ingested.

She was pretty sure Korbin had carried her into the compound over his shoulder and put her to bed in her room. She was surprised she hadn't hit on him, but if he had been carrying her she wouldn't have been in any shape to be throwing out sexual demands.

She poured herself a cup of coffee and sat down at the kitchen table, holding the cup up to her nose. She looked up as Katie came through the door and smiled.

Katie nodded at her and strode over to the coffeemaker,

looking more awake than normal. Stephanie ran through her memories from the night before and tried to figure out where Katie fit into them. The last thing she remembered was Katie on the dance floor with some hottie, but then she got lost in her own desires.

"Where did you go last night?" Stephanie took a sip of her coffee.

"I went four-wheeling with one of the guys from Amy's team," Katie told her nonchalantly. "Then I came back here. I think you guys were already in bed."

"Mmmm, when I got back I was out like a light." Stephanie groaned, eyeing Katie as she took a seat across from her. "That's what shots of tequila and cheap beer do to me. This body is not recovering like my younger version used to, though."

"Cuss out your demon," Katie advised, not making eye contact.

"What's up with you?" Stephanie asked. "You're acting different than normal."

"No, I'm not," she argued, holding back a smile.

"Yes, yes you are. You are acting like you got… No… Did you… *Nooo!*" Stephanie gasped, covering her mouth.

Katie chuckled. "What in the world are you blabbering about?"

Stephanie pointed across the table at Katie. "YOU BITCH! YOU GOT *LAID!*"

"Shhh!" Katie reached over and slapped Stephanie on the hand. "Oh my God, tell the whole fucking world, why don't you? How in the hell did you know that?"

Oh please! Pandora laughed. *Anyone could tell from a mile away. First, you disappeared with a hot guy and didn't come home until the sun came up. Second, you are beaming and have red cheeks, and you're holding back a smirk. Third, you are acting all fluffy and light, like the world revolves around you. Fourth, that bitch was a madam, okay, and she has a sex demon in her. She can smell that shit a mile away. I told you point-blank you were never going to be able to hide it, but nooo! You wanted to act like you were Elizabeth Fucking Taylor.*

I am not acting like that, Katie replied, putting her hand to her cheek. *Am I?*

You are practically screaming at the top of your lungs that you just got some dick. I'm serious; even Korbin would know just by looking at you.

"Okay, tell me all about it," Stephanie demanded, suddenly awake. "Was he hot? Did he have a big...you know?"

"He was more than hot," Katie whispered, giggling. "Muscles for days, blue eyes that almost completely hid his demon circles they were so blue, and yeah, his you know was probably the biggest I've ever encountered."

"Oh my God," Stephanie exclaimed, fanning herself with the napkin. "Did he know how to use it, though? He could have a billy club down there, but if he doesn't know how to use it it's a waste of a man. You just have to throw the whole man away and start over."

Katie giggled through a mouthful of coffee. "No, he definitely knew what he was doing, and it was like he could read my fucking body. It was intense."

"Oh my God, I love it." Stephanie groaned. "You needed to get laid, like seriously. Did you know that while you were gone Korbin asked me out on a date?"

"Really?" Katie exclaimed excitedly. "It's about

damn time."

"I know, right?" Stephanie laughed. "I was such a dipshit, too, I thought he was talking about an incursion, so I'm acting like it's no big thang, telling him I didn't want to get blood on my heels. Then I looked at his face. He was like a puppy dog. That was when I realized... Oh. My. Gosh! He is asking me on a real date. So we went out for Italian, and it was amazing."

"I'm so excited for you guys," Katie told her. "Seriously, you both deserve to be happy, and I've known forever that he had feelings for you. I knew he was scared, though. I'm glad he finally came to his senses and asked you out."

"Me too." Stephanie sighed and sipped her coffee. "Now I just gotta get used to navigating his very complex mind."

Korbin was in his office right after the sun came up and he smiled at his coffee pot, thankful that he decided to install one in his office. He'd had a blast with Stephanie the night before, but she had been wasted when they got home so he'd put her to bed and sat close by, just making sure she was okay. Finally, he had gone to his own room and passed out until the alarm went off. It was going to be a slow day for him, but he was okay with that. He hadn't had one of those in a very long time.

His office phone rang, and he picked it up.

"This is Korbin," he answered.

"Korbin, this is the chief, over at the Los Angeles Police Department." He sounded nervous as hell. "We have a problem."

"What is it, Chief?" Korbin asked, sitting up straight and grabbing a pen.

"We had a call that two gangs were coming together, but then something strange happened out in the hills. We don't really know what is going on, only that people are now missing. We sent a small search party out there first, figuring we would check it out before calling you guys, but they never came back. We heard people screaming into the radios about some kind of monster, then we lost all communication with them. I feel like at this point it is smarter to call you guys than lose a second search team. Those guys were veterans, so if they were screaming about a monster you can be sure as hell there is something out there that is not normal; not even for the hills of Los Angeles."

T'Chezz looked at the drifting souls groaning through the fiery landscape. Moloch sat beside him, chewing on a human leg bone as he leaned back on the bench. He was trying to give T'Chezz some advice, but the demon was struggling to understand what he was trying to tell him. He wanted Moloch's help, there was no doubt about that, but he felt like T'Chezz wasn't listening and it was starting to frustrate him.

"You use brute force, T'Chezz," Moloch told him, smacking his demon lips. "You throw your dregs against their best, but what you need to be thinking about is pitting their best against other humans who can match their skills. Humans who have our interests at heart and allow their demons to direct them. If they have a team hunting us, we should be playing right along with their little game."

"I don't see how that would rid us of the problem," T'Chezz grumbled.

Moloch glanced up from his snack. "Because humans who fully accept enlightenment are much stronger than those forced to do the demon's bidding, even if they are sharing their power with the human. These Enlightened on our side can be the power for you. Your personal hand of the devil."

"I've been working on a plan, though," T'Chezz replied. "I've been setting up these politicians; the rich old white men who pretty much run the world over there. They are slowly taking down their defenses from the inside while my demons crush the military teams in the rural areas."

"Come with me," Moloch ordered, tossing the bone into the lava below and licking his fingers. "I want you to watch something."

Moloch stood up and cracked his knuckles, then waved his hands. T'Chezz watched as a portal began to open right in front of him.

Moloch nodded and walked into the portal, leaving T'Chezz standing there. Finally he went in after him, coming out safely on Earth.

This was why he wanted to move up. Moloch was much more powerful than he was, but he knew he could get to that point.

The system was designed to make the higher demons more powerful. The more levels you climbed, the more powers you possessed. T'Chezz had no doubt in his mind that he could be one of the most powerful of the Seventy-Two.

23

Korbin stood in the training area watching the team packing up their weapons and gear. They were headed for Los Angeles to help in any way they could.

He had a feeling this was going to be a big one, especially since the gangbangers had never returned and the search party had gone missing.

He knew the Chief had been nervous since the last big incident and didn't want to take any chances. He wouldn't have called unless he was almost certain there was an incursion happening.

Los Angeles was a busy place, and densely populated. If word got out, not only would people's lives be in danger, but the media would be all over the damn thing.

Katie shoved two guns into her bag as backup, just in case, and ran her hand over the box of bullets. She had learned to hate big incursions; there was a good chance that not everyone would make it out alive.

Their team was tightly knit, more so than ever before; she couldn't imagine losing one of her teammates. She shoved the thought from her mind. This was her life, and though she had gotten caught up in the other side of things, the reality of it was that she had to deal with this— the potential loss of family.

There were lives at stake; not just theirs, but the lives of those who couldn't protect themselves from the forces that were seeping through the gates of hell.

Anybody else—anybody not familiar with this concept —would scoff at the idea of running off to put your life on the line to help some gangbangers, but not Katie.

She could still vividly remember those boys in the cemetery that night. They had stood strong and fast, trying to help; trying to hold back that demon with their illegal pistols.

She could still see the pile of bodies on the ground; not one of the gang members had walked away from that fight. They may have been caught up in a lifestyle they shouldn't have been, but when it came down to it they were brave. They had stood up for other innocent people, only to lose their lives.

Katie shook her head and shoved the box of bullets into the bag. This wasn't the time for second thoughts.

The team loaded their gear into the helicopter and Korbin took the stick, having spent the last few months flying as much as he could. He didn't have his pilot's license yet, but he didn't have time to wait for the pilot to get there. They needed to get to Los Angeles fast.

"I think we should skip the airport, boss," Calvin suggested as he climbed in.

"I'd have to agree," Derek said, his laptop in his lap. "This one is big, whatever it is, and we don't need to waste time going to one airport and flying to another, only to have to take a car to the scene. It's out there a ways, so our best bet is to fly right to it."

"I agree with you both," Korbin said. "I'd like to have my own ride there; it makes for a quicker exit."

"Very true," Derek agreed, nodding and closing his laptop.

"Except," Korbin grumbled, "no one better throw a gravestone and crash my multi-million-dollar bird."

"If that happens, you will know how I felt when I lost my beautiful baby-blue Ferrari," Katie told him, shaking her head. "It was purely tragic."

"Except we would all die," Eric pointed out.

"Meh, maybe." Katie dismissed the thought. "But if not, you would feel the intense yearning for revenge. Nobody messes with the ride."

"You might be right." Korbin buckled in. "Let's hope we don't have to find out."

Katie nodded, still shaking her head thinking about the loss of her baby.

Sure, she loved her Raptor and wouldn't trade it for the world, but she still thought about her first love—the California T, sitting so shiny on the lot as it waited for her to take it home.

Little did it know its life would be short but meaningful.

Rest in peace. Pandora sighed. *Rest in beautiful baby-blue-Ferrari peace.*

I will avenge her, Katie growled. *Maybe your asshole brother will be there and I can smack him around a bit.*

I really wouldn't wish for that. Pandora shuddered. *I do not feel like facing that hunk of asshole this morning. If he is there, that means the whole farm has come out to fight. We might just be outnumbered.*

The helicopter flew swiftly through the early morning air, heading straight for the coordinates they had been given. Korbin stared out at the scenery as he flew, watching it stream by him. He didn't know what was happening, but he couldn't shake the feeling that something big was about to take place.

He had been on hundreds of calls, but like so many times before, this one felt different. He looked back at the team sitting quietly in their seats staring out the windows. This was his team; his responsibility, and he didn't know if he could take losing another one.

He pushed the thoughts from his head as they reached the scene, which was an old set used for filming westerns about sixty years before.

Korbin slowly took the bird down, avoiding the massive swarm of people on the ground. He was irritated that they were there. This wasn't a game; it was dangerous, and there were way too many cops and police dogs milling around.

They were obviously waiting for the team to arrive, which was good since they didn't need to be running into things alone, but the more people there were—especially those who were not infected—the more chance there was that word would get out about what was going on.

He touched the bird down on the ground and switched off the blades. The team grabbed their bags and moved out quickly.

They knew there was some serious shit going down. Katie was shocked that so many of the LAPD had shown up to fight with them. Korbin was pissed, though; the more attention they got, the angrier he got.

They weren't celebrities. They were demon hunters, and their job was supposed to be top secret, meaning that very few people knew about them. From the looks of things, Katie and Calvin had a real fan club gathered out there. The cops were merely spectators who had come to watch another demon incursion.

"Why are all these people here?" Korbin grumped, pulling his bag out.

"There are high-level demons out here," Calvin replied, shoving his short sword into the sheath at his side. "These cops are just glad they don't have to face it on their own. They know the D Squad now."

"The *what*?" Korbin replied, lifting an eyebrow.

"That's what they call us." Calvin smiled. "We are the Demon Squad, LA chapter."

"Great," Korbin replied, rolling his eyes.

As they came toward the crowd many of the cops started waving and clapping. They stopped in front of the group and Calvin patted Korbin on the shoulder, nodding at Katie. She stepped forward and put her hands up to silence the crowd.

"Everyone, this is a very serious situation," she began. "We are here to help. You all know me and my colleague here, but let me introduce you to our fearless leader Korbin."

Korbin looked around as the crowd erupted into cheers, thankful for what he did. He could feel the anger leave him, and he realized Calvin was right; those men relied on them. They knew that if they went into that situation, none of them would go home to their kids and wives.

They considered them a team of superheroes. Katie put her hands up again and quieted the crowd.

"Who has a 9mm?" Katie asked loudly.

Almost every hand in the crowd went up and Katie smiled. Korbin lifted an eyebrow and looked at Stephanie. She shook her head, letting him know that he needed to just trust wherever this was going. He sighed and turned back to the crowd, knowing she was right. She had, after all, been one of the main people on all of the most recent incursions, while Korbin had spent his time building their new base.

"Now, who is willing to go with us into the brush?" Katie asked.

Korbin looked around as all but three hands went down. Katie nodded and waved those people over. She glanced at the others, who looked almost ashamed for not volunteering.

"Hey, don't give me those looks," she told them. "Every single one of you is vital and important to the protection of this city. You will get to go home to your families tonight, and that is okay with me. I need all of you to stay low and stay prepared for anything, though. Most of you know that these things can spiral out of hand in a heartbeat. I don't want a bunch of cop deaths on this mission. Spread out, and keep your eyes peeled."

Katie went over to the three volunteers and grabbed her bag, pulling out a box. She could tell they were nervous, but she was proud of them for stepping up.

"What are your names?" Katie asked.

"I'm Adam," a dark-haired obvious rookie told her.

"I'm Pescoville," a thirty-something red-headed cop replied.

"I'm Jamie," the third police officer informed Katie. Her hair was pulled back in a tight bun at the base of her neck. "We all work out of the same precinct."

"Thank you, folks. You are seriously appreciated," Katie assured them, handing them each enough bullets for two loads of their pistols. "I want you to get rid of your normal bullets and use these in their place. These are special and rare, so use them sparingly. That being said, do whatever you need to do to get these bastards locked down. I don't want to see any casualties. I want you guys to suit up. You are going to be our second string. If any of these demons get past us, you stop them from going any farther."

"How do we know these bullets will kill the demons?" Jamie asked.

Damian chuckled, walking forward. "We just spent one hell of a day with the military testing these babies out. Trust me, they kill very well."

"You remember what happens when a demon dies?" Katie asked.

They all shook their heads. "They either turn to dust or

they shrivel back up into their human skin, but either way they are dead. Now, does anybody out here have a machete?"

"A machete?" Adam exclaimed, surprised. "We are Los Angeles cops. We don't really run around with machetes, though it might help keep the peace if we did."

"What do you need a machete for?" Jamie asked.

"You might need it to decapitate a demon if the bullet doesn't kill them right away," Katie said, closing her bag and tightening her vest.

"Oh, God." Jamie grimaced. "I think I just threw up in my mouth."

"I used to do that all the time." Katie chuckled as she tightened her bootlaces. "You get used to it after a while. If you don't have anything like that, make sure you pop them right in between the eyes."

Pescoville nodded. "That I can handle."

"Yeah," Jamie agreed. "If it means I don't have to cut anyone's head off, I'll become the best shot you ever saw."

The team started toward the hills, knowing the demons were just on the other side.

They made their way to the top and looked down, watching hordes of demon gangbangers running wildly around, ripping the limbs from the bodies of the members of the search party. The gang members had been duped. They had come for a fight, but their bodies had been taken over before they could even fire their weapons.

Since their souls were already dark the demons had completely taken them over, and only hours after the whole thing had started their faces were barely recognizable. Katie shook her head, pulling out her two short swords and holding them in front of her. She looked down the line and nodded, winking at Derek, who had his knives out and ready.

"All right, team," Korbin yelled. "Let's kick some motherfucking demon ass."

With that the team raced down the hill into the center

of the action, splitting apart and taking different areas. Stephanie jumped over a demon's head and turned quickly, stabbing it in the back of the neck. She turned back just in time to dodge the slashing claws of another demon. Derek and Eric battled through the mass of infected, slicing with their knives and taking as many heads as they could. Katie smiled at Calvin as he pulled a demon's head straight off its body and tossed it over his shoulder. She leaped and spun in the air, kicking three different demons in the back of the head. Their skulls clanked together like wooden stress balls and they dropped to their knees. She severed all three of their heads from their bodies with a few slashes of her sword.

The sounds of pistols firing suddenly caught their attention, but Katie punched another demon in the face and sliced his neck open before pausing to listen. One of the demons must have gotten past them, and the secondary team was on the job. After a few moments, the pistol fire stopped and a roar came from the other side of the hill.

"TAKE THAT, YOU MOTHERFUCKING DEMON FROM HELL!" Katie recognized the voice as Jamie's; she was pretty surprised the tight-ass quiet one had gotten so into it.

Whatever. Pandora scoffed. *Watch your left side.*

Katie thrust her sword into a demon's chest and it turned to dust.

That would be like stepping on a roach and claiming a medal for your "intense actions on the field of battle," Pandora growled. *They are posers; nothing but damn pos— Watch your right side.*

Katie sighed and turned again, this time kicking high in

the air. She hit the demon in the neck, and his bones cracked. His head went all the way to the side, and he flashed into ash as he dropped to the ground.

Ouch. Pandora giggled. *That one would have hurt.*

Seriously, you need to let that shit go, Katie told her, fighting a demon hand to hand. *They are happy to have a chance in this war. There is no place for so many of them in this battle. They are born and bred cops, and nothing else. It's like when we helped out on that bank robbery; it was in my blood to help those people, demons or not. I am just lucky to be strong enough to face both kinds.*

Fine. I'll take it easy on them, but you need to be careful who you bring in, Pandora warned. *They will lose their lives so easily against my brother.*

Aw, look at you! Katie laughed. *Caring about the lives of humans like that.*

Don't start, Pandora snarled. *I don't give a shit about them. I just know that it kills you when there are civilian casualties, and I don't feel like going through another sad sappy emotional rollercoaster with you.*

Mmmhmm. Katie pulled out a knife and threw it as hard as she could into the back of a demon's head. *I won't tell your secret.*

I hate you, Pandora growled.

Katie laughed and ran forward to catch the knife in midair as the demon dissolved around it. Stephanie looked over and nodded at Katie before turning back and ripping a demon's throat out with her bare hands.

Katie was pretty impressed by that and wondered if she could do the same. She shrugged continued battling through the plethora of demons, trying to make a dent in the chaos. She didn't know where they had all come from, but then she didn't care. She just needed to make sure they stayed there until they died. She cut the head off another demon and briefly watched Derek as he battled two smaller ones.

He laughed as he threw kicks and punches, almost toying with the damn things. Katie smirked, knowing it must have felt good for Derek to get out of the computer room and get back into the fight. He was out of practice, but he seemed to have no problem holding his own.

She liked having him there. He was family; family from way back.

Katie turned and leaped into the air, letting a charging demon go right under her. When she landed she tapped the demon on his shoulder. He turned around growling, the teardrop tattoo from the human he had taken over still visible on his scaly black cheek.

She took a step forward and pulled out her pistols, feeling like an Old West gunslinger. She pulled both triggers at the same time, blowing holes in the demon's stomach.

She laughed as he turned to dust, then turned around to see what Derek was doing. As she turned he looked at her and smiled. Katie smiled back, but her eyes shifted past him to the two large demons stomping forward with their guns pointed at Derek and the demons he was fighting.

As if in slow motion, Katie screamed and pointed. Derek turned back around as the demons opened fire. Derek took bullet after bullet, his arms flying into the air and his weapons falling from his hands to hit the ground behind him.

Katie screamed again, unable to get through the pile of demons in her way fast enough.

The large beasts in front of Derek just kept shooting until there were no more bullets left in their weapons. They pressed the triggers over and over, and the clicks echoed in Katie's brain.

Derek was on the ground, and the two he had been fighting were nothing but dust.

Derek clenched his fingers on the grass beneath him and groaned loudly as the large demons came forward, stopping at his feet. He lifted his hand to shoot, but his weapon was gone. He dropped his hand and looked up at the sky; the pain was almost unbearable.

Katie ran across the field toward Derek, slicing with her swords and screaming in anger. Her eyes flashed bright red and her fists were clenched around her weapons' hilts.

When she had cleared the masses a bit she shoved her swords back into their sheaths. The two large demons had left Derek alone and moved into the crowd to fight with the others, but at that moment Katie was only concerned with getting to Derek's side.

She slid to her knees next to him and looked his body over. There were multiple bullets embedded in his vest, but on his side, where the armor didn't cover, were multiple bullet holes.

She pushed her palm over the wounds and closed her eyes for a moment, not wanting to go through what she knew she was about to. Tears streamed down her face and she pulled him into her lap, holding him in her arms.

He spoke, softly, with a slight whistle in his voice. "Tell

Korbin the password for the servers is 'KatieIsHott.'" He looked up to her eyes and smiled. "'Hott' with two Ts."

Katie sobbed a laugh and he chuckled, then curled into a tight fetal position. Blood spewed from his mouth and ran down his chin, but he didn't panic. He just stared into Katie's eyes, feeling like he was exactly where he needed to be. The battle raged around them but Katie tuned it out, not wanting to be bothered. She trusted Pandora to warn her.

"You're gonna be okay," she told him through tears. "Just hold on and let your demon heal you."

"No." He shook his head and whispered, "He's already gone; done what he could. That was a big bullet, dude."

Katie laughed through her tears and shook her head. She wouldn't let him go. She *couldn't* let him go. She rubbed her hand over his cheek and leaned forward to kiss him on the forehead.

"We have so much to do," Katie told him. "There's so much exploring that we still haven't done. You have to pull through this. It's not your time yet."

"It is." He reached up and moved a piece of hair from her cheek. "And it's okay, because I am ready for it. I'll finally get to read a fucking book."

"I'll read you a book," she cried, feeling his breathing getting shallower by the second. "I'll read you every goddamn book we have, and I'll buy more. You just have to stay with me. We can help you."

"It's okay." He smiled and touched her wet cheek. "I want you to do something for me. I want you to bury my ashes…in the dirt up….on the mountain where we saw… the sunset. Will you do that?"

She nodded, unable to speak or move from that spot. She held him in her arms as he turned his eyes up to the clouds. The light from the sun flooded down over them—just them—at that moment.

"Please," she sobbed, putting her head next to his. "Please don't do this, Derek. Please don't go."

When she raised her head he was gone; the last of the air had left his lungs. She screamed and threw her head back, wiping her face on her sleeve.

She closed his eyes and kissed him one last time on the forehead.

She carefully laid his body on the ground and got herself to her feet. Her hands squeezed tightly around the grips of her guns, and as she lifted her head her eyes shone painfully bright.

She screamed again, but her voice was deep and menacing; there was pain in the tone. She ran toward the large demon who had killed Derek and jumped onto its back, pressing the barrel of her gun against its head.

"Fuck you," she whispered as she pulled the trigger.

She jumped off as the beast went down. He instantly turned to dust, but it wasn't good enough for Katie; she wanted it to suffer. She found the other one and slowly walked toward it, firing into its arms and chest. The beast fell to the ground wailing but she continued to shoot, emptying her clip and slamming in the next one while screaming at the top of her lungs.

"GET UP! RESURRECT YOURSELF, MOTHERFUCKER, SO I CAN KILL YOU AGAIN!"

"Hey," Korbin ran up behind her and wrapped his arms around her shoulders. "Shhh… Let it go."

"Oh God," she sobbed, dropping her pistols to the ground and falling to her knees.

Korbin went with her, glancing at Derek's body. He understood now what had happened. He buried his face in her hair and just held her, letting her cry in his arms.

He could feel her pain, and it took everything he had not to lose it himself.

25

The base was silent, even the wind had died down to a gentle breeze. The house was quiet; everyone had found a place to deal with their grief.

When they got back Katie couldn't sleep, so she roamed the tunnels until the sun finally came up and found herself sitting on a rock outside of the perimeter fence. She pulled her legs up to her chin and stared out over the horizon, her thoughts jumbled with the sadness that sat like a boulder in her chest.

"Hey, kid," Damian called as he walked up. He sat down next to her.

She didn't say anything at first, just kept her gaze staring on the hills in the distance. Damian leaned back on the rock and looked at the sky, trying to find the right words.

He had seen her lose it—everyone had—but they understood. They knew that Derek had been important to her. He had been important to everyone.

"How are you doing?" Damian asked.

She wiped her tears on her sleeve and shook her head. "Noah died," she told him. "Noah Rappley from Amy's Assassins. They called me this morning and let me know he paid his tribute in an ambush with a bunch of innocents. He died almost at the same time Derek did. Three others from Amy's team are in critical condition."

A tear fell down her cheek and she sniffled hard, trying not to let the grief take her again. Damian sighed and wrapped his arms around her. She turned her face into his shoulder and cried for minutes, finally pushing back enough to catch her breath. She shook her head against him, not understanding why everything had gotten so hard so fast.

"It's worse now," she sobbed. "The demons; they are coming out of nowhere and killing everyone. How are we supposed to protect the innocents if we can't keep ourselves safe? I was just out with Noah a few days ago, laughing and having a hell of a time. He talked about a real life—one with people he loved—and that was starting to include me."

"Shhh," Damian whispered holding her tightly for a moment before drawing back. "I know this is hard to take in. It's all happened so suddenly."

"Everything in our lives is fucking sudden!" she burst out. "There are no easy goodbyes, if such a thing even exists. There are no warning signs or illnesses. Derek looked at me and smiled, then turned around and took a dozen bullets to the body. He thought everything was going to be okay, and in the blink of an eye he was taking his last breath. I'm just tired of saying goodbye. I'm so fucking *tired* of it."

"I know." Damian sighed. "But that is the way it is for us. There are a million hellos, and just as many goodbyes. I have to go check on the others, but if you need anything—anything at all—you come find me, okay?"

"Yeah." She sighed. "Thank you. I'll get it together, I promise."

Damian leaned forward and kissed her on the forehead before getting up and walking back toward the gate. Katie watched him go, knowing that one day her tears would be for him—if she didn't get it first. She closed her eyes and tilted her head toward the sun, thinking about that night with Noah. Thinking about watching the sunrise with him, how secure she had felt in his strong arms. It had been an illusion, one that she had fallen straight into.

You know, I don't usually tell people this, but I've been married more times than I can count, Pandora began. *And definitely for longer than any human woman ever could be. None of them ever ended well for me, though. I was not the woman they thought, and I had to watch them die. I adopted the policy that I would love them and leave them.*

"I just don't know how I can deal with another death like this," Katie admitted, speaking out loud. "It grinds me to the soul. The first ones…they were hard, but I think my body was in shock. These two—they have brought me to my knees."

I know. I don't know how you feel, but I know you can't continue to take this over and over. The human body is fragile, but the most fragile part of it all is something I can't see or fix. Your heart—not the physical beating organ, but the heart that loves, that cares, that feels. Demons can't touch it. You took chances and opened your heart as a sister to Derek and as a lover to Noah, and I'm sorry you lost them both in one night. I wish I could have seen that coming; to have prepared you somehow.

"The crazy thing is, I don't even know if I would have made a different choice with Noah. Being that close to him opened up a lot of things in me that had closed when I became Damned. For the first time, I felt secure in someone else's arms. For that brief moment in time, I was safe from everything in the world."

But you weren't, Pandora replied. *I know the feeling was there, but you* weren't *safe. None of us will be until we can end all this. You loved and lost, and I'm sorry for that.*

Katie stood up from the rock and rolled her shoulders, wrapping her arms around her chest. She could feel the pain thumping in her stomach, and her tears just wouldn't stop.

"My love will be hot, and burn with them for a night," Katie exclaimed. "Perhaps another time in the future we will have the chance to enjoy relationships that last longer. But if not, at least for one night of passion, everything will be right in the world."

Amen, Pandora whispered.

This time the bar wasn't loud and boisterous.

It was a little emptier and a lot more solemn, and the pictures of Noah and Derek stared directly into Katie's soul.

The three critical-cares from Amy's team were still in

the hospital, and the loss of two veteran hunters had really hit the teams hard. There wasn't a dry eye in the place by the time Katie took the stage.

She had done this many times now—paid tribute to the fallen, read the poem, and brought them all back together again—but she felt like the thread that stitched the wound had finally started to unravel. She wasn't even sure how she was supposed to get out of her seat, but she had to.

"You ready?" Korbin whispered in her ear. "You think you can do this?"

Katie looked up at Korbin, then over at the two pictures. She *had* to do it. Those men deserved the same strong send-off as all the others, and it had become her place to do it.

She nodded and pushed her chair back, smiling at Korbin as he helped her up. Everyone went silent as she walked toward the stage, alone in the spotlight.

With each step she thought about the first time she had really talked to Derek, outside that sex shop when she was first Damned. He was so funny; such a loner, but he was a really great guy, and much loved.

Katie reached the top of the stairs and walked over to the mic, which was now situated at a podium.

They were moving up in the world.

She took the old crinkled piece of paper from her pocket and set it on the stand as she cleared her throat. She looked past the crowd as the door opened and General Brushwood and Colonel Jehovivich, dressed in civilian clothes, walked in. They took a seat at the table with Korbin and the others, and the general nodded at Katie.

She felt that if nothing else, in this war she had helped

bring the military together with the mercs, and that was very important.

"Today we pay tribute to the fallen," Katie said into the mic. "I had the honor of being with Derek Tosh when he took his last breath. I held him in my arms, wondering how we had gotten that far; how we had come to a moment when the demons were just too much. I don't have an answer to that yet. Derek was a calm and comforting man, always there for others, always smiling, and always laughing at the silly memes he searched for on his phone. He liked to be alone, but when he was with his family he truly shined. May the angels carry him into the light, and may he ever rest in peace and honor. I only knew Noah Rappley for a few days before he passed away, but I can tell you that he was a force to be reckoned with. His team-mates remember him as a dreamer, a man full of hope and love for the future. He was a Viking on the field and a big teddy bear with his friends and family. Noah will be missed in my heart and others."

Katie sighed and looked down at the sheet in front of her, knowing it was time to once again read the poem.

"We are the chosen.
The infected,
battling our demons night and day.
Protecting the uninformed from reality.
We fight where the stupid meet the clueless to
perform the asinine for our
teammates every day.
We are cops, military, special forces, and SWAT,
medical techs, priests, and clergy.

We are the dimensional derelicts,
the legion, the host, the forgotten.
The *feared*.
The sheep can sleep at night because we don't.
We fight for humanity—yours—and for our own.
We are the Damned, and death is our enemy,
our escape,
and our *tribute*.

"Thank you."

The people in the crowd clapped between their tears, and Katie stepped down and made her way back to the table. As she approached, the general stood up and reached out his hand to shake hers.

"I'm sorry for your loss."

"Thank you, General."

"I am more than appreciative of the rounds—the gifts that you gave us. They have already saved lives," the general told her.

Katie sat down next to him and ordered some nachos from the waitress. The general ordered some food as well, and took a big swallow of his beer.

"I think that I might be able to help you and your team," the general suggested. "I think we should sit down tomorrow and talk about it."

"That would be great." Katie smiled. "We can definitely do that. We need to move on...that is for sure."

The general nodded and they turned to the others, listening to them talk about Derek and all the funny jokes he used to tell.

Katie smiled and chuckled as she listened to Eric talk

about him, especially since Eric had become so close to Derek.

Her heart went out to him; to him and everyone else on the team. When the food arrived they dug in, their spirits and voices lifted. A fight broke out suddenly to their left, and everyone on the team grabbed their food and beers and held them in the air. The general and the colonel, however, were too busy watching the fight, and sat wide-eyed as the two fighters tussled and slammed into their table.

Katie tried to hold back her laughter as cheese and French fries flew everywhere. The general and the colonel looked at the others and realized they were holding their food in the air. The two guys slowly picked themselves up off the floor, and the larger one peeled the general's basket of cheese fries off his thigh.

"I think this is yours," he said, handing it to the general.

"Thanks." He just shook his head.

The bartender rushed over and set down another table, and Katie signaled to the waitress to bring more food. Everyone burst into laughter, and even the general and the colonel couldn't keep straight faces.

Somehow it always ended with a laugh.

WRITTEN APRIL 13, 2018

Ok, "la la la" thanks for reading and all of that shit he normally puts in the first paragraph. I'm sure you all like reading it every time he writes it, but I'm a bit cross at the moment.

Korbin bought potato flour-based donuts and they fucking suck in the morning when you try to reheat them. Just sayin'.

There, *that's* why I'm bitchy, you *nosy* individual.

Well, that, and I'm apparently 'The Author's' little play-toy for these *Author Notes*. I wrote *Author Notes* for the last book, and so now we have another chronicle of our ongoing lives coming out tomorrow. He asked me nicely, so I said I would be happy to do them.

<Michael edit: Did not say anything about happy. She said I owed her food.>

I didn't promise The Author I'd be nice in these author notes, but I'll *try*.

First, THANK YOU for reviewing our books! We are

up to a hundred and forty-nine reviews on Book One (500+ people in the group, but I digress) which is about seven hundred fucking reviews too few, so get off your human asses and go put up a review. If you do anything less than a 5*, I will *absolutely* visit you in your dreams. If you *DO* put up a five star, then I will visit you in your dreams but with a totally different outcome.

(Well, damn. I'm told I can't use threats to get reviews, because blah blah blah... So, "Would you kindly consider placing a review on these books? The authors earn better positioning within the Amazon algorithms due to how often, how recent, and how good the reviews are.")

<OMG – I think I'm going to *HURL* now. Or better yet, make Katie hurl. That was so damned sappy! My first suggestion to get reviews was to offer <redacted> or <redacted> but I'm told we could be <redacted> with a hot poker if I did that.>

So, Katie finally got some <redacted> and let me tell you, it was absolutely good for me...I mean *her*. Whatever. *What is good for me is good for her.*

Then the little twerp she had the hots for had to go and get offed by (I suspect) an asshole who isn't my brother. My brother (from a different mother) is an *idiot*. I've not exactly clued Katie into it, but if he was running the show my time on Earth would be a vacation. If <redacted> is starting to play too? Well, I think the vacation might be over.

OH! Have you seen the latest on the soap opera? I can't believe that hussy really spread the welcome wagon like she did. For what? It wasn't like he was enhanced enough in the right department to <redacted> the <redacted>. I have *NO* clue what she saw in him. Coming from a person who knows how to grade prime man-meat, she really went to the bargain bin that holds day-old meat to find *him*. I suspect she could have done better by going to a corner and offering to sell potato chips...

You know...*Lays for a $1.00?*

Don't groan, Katie cuts me off with these jokes. You are a captive audience who can't talk back (except in reviews... hehehehehe) or on the Facebook group, I suppose. But since I'm not placing the link to the Protected by the Damned Facebook Group in these *Author Notes*, you can *suck it.*

<Looking down at my notes on what Sir *Jackass* wants me to write about...>

So, we have two more books about us coming out in the next four weeks. Tell your family and friends about these stories.

I'm told I can't require or even suggest you buy them for young adults, because that will cause their heads to spin about on the axes of their necks until they pop off.

I still don't understand why that's a problem. Seems like good entertainment to me.

I've got my eyes on two more crotches for Katie...Uh, two more "heart throbs," but she can be pretty fucking annoying in the "no" department. She needs to say yes more often and just let the future ride.

And ride...and ride...and <Damn... I need a fan.>

Speaking of Sir Jackass, it says here that he will be meeting with Lady Hair-by-Electrical-Socket next week to work on the Melneck stuff. He's a pain in the ass (Melneck, not Sir Jackass... Although Jackass is too.) However,

Melneck IS a lot more powerful than his ranking suggests; he just doesn't play politics worth a damn.

And is smart enough to know how not to piss off those who do.

Ok, I've passed the seven hundred and fifty words now. *WHERE THE FUCK ARE MY DONUTS, JACKASS?*

Lovingly,

Pandora

Well, hello! Hope you enjoyed that action packed, funny, donut-loving, chicken nugget enjoying story. Can't get much better than Pandora and Katie. Not for a good chuckle, eye roll, or heart-racing good time.

It's been crazy around here, but I'm thinking you knew that.

I've been working hard on this project with Mike, our 7sons projects, and my cozy mystery. And of course, ROMANCE. I know you guys might not all read romance, but my Ali and Weston Parker lines are the majority of our focus.

Why romance?

I'm a sucker for a good redemption story, and while I know that can happen in any story, it's usually the central theme in my romance novels. Take the most broken, "fuck love and its fruity colors and hearts" guy and pair him up with a strong, independent woman, and I just have fun.

Trying to get the two of them to grow and compromise is the name of the game.

Now, if I'm being honest, I'm a SUCKER for a paranormal romance, though that's not what I write. There have been a few stories (contemporary romances) when I got to the point of wanting a vamp to jump out and slay the whole cast and crew, but I refrained.

I also just released my fifth book in my Zodiac series under WL Knightly. That's with a good friend of mine, and we just wanted to write some scary-ass mystery slasher novels—so we did! It's been a fun ride. I'm shocked as hell that we're almost halfway through the thirteen-book series. It's a book a month on that one too.

Outside of that, we've been to Illinois and Missouri to help a friend through surgery and to eat at the buffet the college of the Ozarks kids put on a few times in the last few weeks. I've gained three pounds thanks to the all-you-can-eat function of the buffet, but such is life. Padding is a good thing—I think. If not, don't tell me.

I formed my first JIT team to read over my cozy mystery chapters that are finished, and we've had a damn good time with those readers. Everyone has peed themselves, spit coke from their noses, or laughed to tears. I'm thinking my old ladies in that cozy mystery are going to lift some spirits and give a few people a break from the routine that is life at times.

That's what good books do. They take us away. At least, we hope they do. Best way (in my opinion) to have an adventure. As such, I sure as hell hope you had a GREAT adventure with this last book. Mike is in charge of the antics and titles—they just couldn't be any better. He's a brilliant guy with a fun, light-hearted demeanor. If you get the chance to meet him, don't pass it up. It's worth the trip–I promise.

And with that, I want to say thank you again for picking up the novel and reading these author notes. I feel like it's giving you a quick look into our diary. I'm an introvert, so I'm thinking I might have to start making shit up soon to stay fresh, relevant and fun, but that time has yet to arrive. Appreciate you guys. We do what we do for readers like you.

Slave to many stories,

Laurie Starkey

CONNECT WITH MICHAEL TODD

Want more?

Find us On Facebook

BOOKS BY MICHAEL TODD

PROTECTED BY THE DAMNED

Torn Asunder (01)

Killing Is My Business (02)

And Business Is Good (03)

Sit Down, Shut Up, And Pull The Trigger (04)

Welcome To The Jungle (05)

Metal Up Your Ass (06)

For a complete list of Michael's Kurtherian Gambit Universe books please click this link.

Kurtherian Gambit Series Titles Include:

FIRST ARC

Death Becomes Her (01) - Queen Bitch (02) - Love Lost (03) - Bite This (04) - Never Forsaken (05) - Under My Heel (06) - Kneel Or Die (07)

SECOND ARC

We Will Build (08) - It's Hell To Choose (09) - Release The Dogs of War (10) - Sued For Peace (11) - We Have Contact (12) - My Ride is a Bitch (13) - Don't Cross This Line (14)

THIRD ARC

Never Submit (15) - Never Surrender (16) - Forever Defend (17) - Might Makes Right (18) - Ahead Full (19) - Capture Death (20) - Life Goes On (21)

THE SECOND DARK AGES

with Ell Leigh Clarke

The Dark Messiah (01) - The Darkest Night (02) - Darkest Before The Dawn (03) - Dawn Arrives (04)

THE BORIS CHRONICLES

with Paul C. Middleton

Evacuation (01) - Retaliation (02) - Revelations (03) - Redemption (04)

RECLAIMING HONOR

with Justin Sloan

Justice Is Calling (01) - Claimed By Honor (02) - Judgement Has Fallen (03) - Angel of Reckoning (04) - Born Into Flames (05) - Defending The Lost (06) - Saved By Valor (07) - Return of Victory (08)

THE ETHERIC ACADEMY

with TS Paul

ALPHA CLASS (01) - ALPHA CLASS: Engineering (02)

with N.D. Roberts

Discovery (03)

TERRY HENRY "TH" WALTON CHRONICLES

with Craig Martelle

Nomad Found (01) - Nomad Redeemed (02) - Nomad Unleashed (03) - Nomad Supreme (04) - Nomad's Fury (05) - Nomad's Justice (06) - Nomad Avenged (07) - Nomad Mortis (08) - Nomad's Force (09) - Nomad's Galaxy (10)

TRIALS AND TRIBULATIONS

with Natalie Grey

Risk Be Damned (01) - Damned to Hell (02)

~THE AGE OF MAGIC~

THE RISE OF MAGIC

with CM Raymond and LE Barbant

Restriction (01) - Reawakening (02) - Rebellion (03) - Revolution (04) - Unlawful Passage (05) - Darkness Rises (06) - The Gods Beneath (07) - Reborn (08)

THE HIDDEN MAGIC CHRONICLES

with Justin Sloan

Shades of Light (01) - Shades of Dark (02) - Shades of Glory (03) - Shades of Justice (04)

STORMS OF MAGIC

with PT Hylton

Storm Raiders (01) - Storm Callers (02) - Storm Breakers (03) - Storm Warrior (04)

TALES OF THE FEISTY DRUID

with Candy Crum

The Arcadian Druid (01) - The Undying Illusionist (02) - The Frozen Wasteland (03) - The Deceiver (04) - The Lost (05) - The Damned (06) - Into The Maelstrom (07)

PATH OF HEROES

with Brandon Barr

Rogue Mage (01)

A NEW DAWN

with Amy Hopkins

Dawn of Destiny (01) - Dawn of Darkness (02) - Dawn of Deliverance (03) - Dawn of Days (04) - Broken Skies (05)

TALES OF THE WELLSPRING KNIGHT

with P.J. Cherubino

Knight's Creed (01) - Knight's Struggle (02) - Knight's Justice (03)

~THE AGE OF MADNESS~

LIVE FREE OR DIE

with Haley Lawson

Unleashing Madness (01)

~THE AGE OF EXPANSION~

THE ASCENSION MYTH

*with Ell Leigh Clarke *

Awakened (01) - Activated (02) - Called (03) - Sanctioned (04) - Rebirth (05) - Retribution (06) - Cloaked (07) - Bourne (08) - Committed (09)

CONFESSIONS OF A SPACE ANTHROPOLOGIST

with Ell Leigh Clarke

Giles Kurns: Rogue Operator (01) - Giles Kurns: Rogue Instigator (02)

THE UPRISE SAGA

*with Amy Duboff *

Covert Talents (01) - Endless Advance (02) - Veiled Designs (03) - Dark Rivals (04)

BAD COMPANY

with Craig Martelle

The Bad Company (01) - Blockade (02) - Price of Freedom (03) - (04) Liberation

THE GHOST SQUADRON

with Sarah Noffke

Formation (01) - Exploration (02) - Evolution (03) - Degeneration (04) - Impersonation (05) - Recollection (06)

VALERIE'S ELITES

with Justin Sloan and PT Hylton

Valerie's Elites (01) - Death Defied (02) - Prime Enforcer (03) Justice Earned (04)

SHADOW VANGUARD

with Tom Dublin

Gravity Storm (01)

ETHERIC ADVENTURES: ANNE AND JINX

with S.R. Russell

Etheric Recruit (01) - Etheric Researcher (02)

Other Books

with Craig Martelle & Justin Sloan

Gateway to the Universe

~THE REVELATIONS OF ORICERAN~

THE LEIRA CHRONICLES

with Martha Carr

Waking Magic (01) - Release of Magic (02) - Protection of Magic (03) - Rule of Magic (04) - Dealing in Magic (05) - Theft of Magic (06) - Enemies of Magic (07) - Guardians of Magic (08)

THE UNBELIEVABLE MR. BROWNSTONE

Feared by Hell (01) - Rejected by Heaven (02)

SHORT STORIES

You Don't Touch John's Cousin: Frank Kurns Stories of the UnknownWorld 01 (7.5)

Bitch's Night Out: Frank Kurns Stories of the UnknownWorld 02 (9.5)

with Natalie Grey

Bellatrix: Frank Kurns Stories of the Unknownworld 03 (13.25)

Challenges: Frank Kurns Stories of the Unknownworld 04

AudioBooks

Available at Audible.com and iTunes

CLICK HERE TO SEE ALL LMBPN BOOKS ON AUDIBLE